CAPE
FEVER

CAPE FEVER

NADIA DAVIDS

SCRIBNER

London · New York · Amsterdam/Antwerp · Sydney/Melbourne · Toronto · New Delhi

First published in the United States by Simon & Schuster, LLC, 2025

This edition published in Great Britain by Scribner,
an imprint of Simon & Schuster UK Ltd, 2026

Copyright © 2025 Nadia Davids

SCRIBNER and design are registered trademarks of The Gale Group, Inc.,
used under licence by Simon & Schuster Inc.

The right of Nadia Davids to be identified as author of this work has been
asserted in accordance with the Copyright, Designs and Patents Act, 1988.

For more than 100 years, Simon & Schuster has championed authors and the stories they create. By respecting the copyright of an author's intellectual property, you enable Simon & Schuster and the author to continue publishing exceptional books for years to come. We thank you for supporting the author's copyright by purchasing an authorized edition of this book. No amount of this book may be reproduced or stored in any format, nor may it be uploaded to any website, database, language-learning model, or other repository, retrieval, or artificial intelligence system without express permission. All rights reserved. Inquiries may be directed to Simon & Schuster, 222 Gray's Inn Road, London WC1X 8HB or
RightsMailbox@simonandschuster.co.uk

Simon & Schuster strongly believes in freedom of expression and stands against
censorship in all its forms. For more information, visit BooksBelong.com.

1 3 5 7 9 10 8 6 4 2

Simon & Schuster UK Ltd, 1st Floor
222 Gray's Inn Road, London WC1X 8HB

Simon & Schuster Australia, Sydney
Simon & Schuster India, New Delhi

www.simonandschuster.co.uk
www.simonandschuster.com.au
www.simonandschuster.co.in

A CIP catalogue record for this book is available from the British Library

Hardback ISBN: 978-1-3985-4404-8
eBook ISBN: 978-1-3985-4405-5
eAudio ISBN: 978-1-3985-4406-2

The authorised representative in the EEA is Simon & Schuster Netherlands BV,
Herculesplein 96, 3584 AA Utrecht, Netherlands. info@simonandschuster.nl

This book is a work of fiction.
Names, characters, places and incidents are either a product of the author's
imagination or are used fictitiously. Any resemblance to actual people
living or dead, events or locales is entirely coincidental.

Printed and Bound in the UK using 100% Renewable Electricity at CPI Group (UK) Ltd

*For my grandmothers, Amina and Mary.
And for their mothers.*

CAPE FEVER

PART I

ONE

23 Heron Place
The Cape
Southern Cross Colony
March 12, 1920

I come highly recommended to Mrs. Hattingh through sentences I tell her I cannot read. She conducts the interview in her kitchen, a large room on a street of houses grand and gabled that look out onto the dipped bowl of our harbor city. A row of homes, my father told me, for doctors and ambassadors. When she says the position is for a combined cleaner-cook, I realize she is not as wealthy as her house—its address and ornaments—suggests. I glance past the kitchen door to the corridor, and though the light is dim I notice rows of variously sized rectangles, solid blocks of deep maroon, shades darker than the rest of the wallpaper. Paintings must once have hung there. Perhaps she has had to sell them, and now the memory of each casts a precise and permanent shadow. It is likely she lost part of her fortune in the war. Well, who hasn't? Even those of us who had no fortune to begin with have felt the pinch and scrape and cost of all those trenches and guns and explosions. The kitchen, however, is still well equipped. In the end, as my mother would say, it is the pots, not the paintings, that survive.

So here we are, in the room in which I will be expected to collude in her deceits, concoct dishes for dinner parties that hide her poverty, mind the number of eggs, keep up appearances. I can do that. I am used to culinary economy, to careful pride.

She is holding the letter up to a wide window, squinting with effort as though the words will unfurl in the morning light. The paper is thin as a breeze, the writing as spidery as my previous employer Mrs. Edenburg's spite.

Mrs. Hattingh asks me the usual questions, her voice now firm, now breathless. "How old are you, girl?"

"Nineteen, madam."

"You look younger. I suppose it is because you are so slight. How long have you been in service?"

"Since I was twelve, madam. First as a scullery maid and then as Cook's helper."

"Why did you leave the Edenburgs? Such a glowing reference, I can't imagine why they'd let you go."

To this I say that Cook had never liked me, that she'd wanted my position for her own daughter, that she'd connived to get rid of me! I touch a finger to my lips; days ago, it had been swollen to a bloody pout, but it's calmed since, just a small bump now, dark and tender. *Don't worry,* my mother had said when she first saw it, *the mouth heals quickly.*

"I do hope she taught you to cook before all this intrigue?" Around Mrs. Hattingh's mouth a smile dances.

"Oh yes, madam. I helped Cook for three years. She taught me the settlers' dishes and my mother taught me our food."

"But how wonderful! Can you make that lovely spiced mince dish with dried mint . . . *kee* . . . *kee* . . . the name escapes me now."

"Keema. Yes, madam."

"What about the almond dessert with rose water? And cardamom doughnuts?"

I nod.

"*Excellent*. We shall get along famously. I always hire your people if I can help it, Soraya. I've long admired the skilled cleverness of your men and the industriousness and modesty of your women, even if some say the former is merely cunning and the latter crippling shyness."

"Yes, madam. Thank you, madam."

"In fact"—she leans forward and drops her voice even though there is no one about to hear us—"I feel a kinship with your people. You are not really from here either. Yes, yes, brought by force where we came by design, but still, like us, your kind made this colony what it is."

Ah, she's one of *those*, the ones who think themselves infinitely better than us and us somewhat better than the others, and believes that sharing this will inspire my loyalty, hard work, thankfulness. My mother—herself descended in part from the First People Mrs. Hattingh so easily dismisses—would have given one of her stock responses, such as *We are hard workers indeed*, but I say nothing. Let her make of that what she may.

Mrs. Hattingh also asks some unusual questions.

"Do you think you'll be happy here?"

"Yes, madam."

"You won't mind such an empty house?"

I have to stop a laugh running free from my throat, for what servant would prefer more people to clean up after?

"Would you like to have a look around before you give your answer?"

I shake my head, because, really, there is nothing else to see; the wage is fair, the house large but mostly vacant, and, more, there is no man about to trouble us.

It is only then that she announces that the position is for a live-in maid. Her voice quavers as she reveals this, and I know that *she* knows this is an unreasonable request, sprung late. Neither of us needs state that to sleep here is to be not only cook and cleaner but companion and protector too. I protest (very faintly) that 23 Heron Place is not far from my family's home in the Quarter, that I could come to her early each morning and would not leave until my duties for the day are fulfilled. At this she dips her chin like a small, frail bird, her lips tremble, her hands reach for her long, swaying necklace that runs all the way to her waist. She clutches and rolls the garnet beads lying gleaming and purple against her dark dress as though she were praying and does not answer me directly; instead, she turns her eyes to the back garden and whispers something about holiday half pay. I understand then that my nights are a condition of employment, that she wants my sleeping hours as well as my waking ones, that there is only one answer to secure the job, and so I give it: I will sleep here every night of the week and go home but one Sunday a fortnight.

Her head snaps up, and with a full smile she tells me how much safer she feels already, just knowing I will be here.

My face twitches into a sneer that I try to still. My mother gave me just two lessons before I set out to my first job all those years ago, and I am already failing at one of them: The first was to do as I was told as well as I could, to wash, cook and clean as though I were caring for my own home and person. The second was how to arrange my face. *Always keep something back*, she told me, *there is no need for them to know what you are truly thinking.*

So I do not tell Mrs. Hattingh that I am useless in a crisis, have never bested anyone in self-defense and have no intention of shielding her at any cost to myself against marauding burglars or mountain baboons. She rises to her feet and announces that she will give me a tour of the house and steps into a quick march as I trail after her. At each door we pause, and she names the room behind it. The breathy voice has turned no-nonsense: "Pantry, dining room, sitting room, guest room, gun room, my late husband's study."

She speaks and walks at such a speed that words and feet seem to trip up on each other. The pace, I realize, is because this is all so unbearable, for this is not something that would ordinarily fall to her. In a house of this size, for a family of this station, it should be the task of the housekeeper, not the employer, to show the new housemaid what's what.

But Mrs. Hattingh is forging ahead—almost as if she were another person now, made brisk by the business of it all. She points, and as she does so, she instructs: "You will dust daily, the windows must be washed once a week. You see how very tall they are? This house has wonderful light, but as with every bit of good fortune, it extracts its price, for all is visible, every speck of dust and dirt, and I must warn you, I am *eagle*-eyed. My linen must be changed every fortnight and the floors scrubbed weekly. Mind you work *with* the grain, not against it, or you'll do irreparable damage. These are yellowwood." She taps a toe to a floor plank. "My late husband, Mr. Hattingh, took very seriously the preservation of the Cape's good homes."

A turn, a swish of that long, flounced skirt and the rustling petticoat beneath it, and down the corridor we go. She twists her head over her shoulder, her words small darting fish.

"Be careful with my things, please, I cannot bear the habitual breaking of plates and ornaments that every maid seems guilty of. And remember this: if such breakage does occur after we've quarreled, I will know it to be deliberate." A sharp left. "Always knock before you enter any room and wait a moment for my response. If I don't answer, you may assume I am not there and open the door. Answer the butcher's knock only when I tell you to. I do not keep a telephone—a boastful extravagance in any home—so I will ask you to carry messages to my friends as needed. *Walk*, my dear, you should not have such a languid gait at your age. Up the stairs now. March on."

She trails her pale fingers on the oak banister as she ascends the stairs, and I find myself thinking of my mother's hands. Mama had me when she was seventeen, and when I look at Mrs. Hattingh, I can see easily who is younger by the face, but their hands are different. My mother rubs her palms and nails nightly with the oil she buys from the Indian shopkeeper in the District, but by day her skin cracks at the knuckles, ash gray against brown. It's the lye in the soap that does it. She's one of many washerwomen in the Quarter who spend their days cleaning, scrubbing, soaking things for the city's grand and not-so-grand houses. All day, all day, wash-wash, scrub-scrub, soak-soak, clothes, linen, curtains, soiled nappies for babies and the infirm. She works like a soldier, my mother, rising early, sleeping late, setting her teeth as though she's going into battle when she leaves for the washhouse. She does it even though my father turns a respectable trade because she refuses to believe that religious calligraphy will ever provide enough for the body despite what it may do for the soul.

CAPE FEVER

Mrs. Hattingh's joints are slender where Mama's are knotted. Against the oak, my new employer's fingers have the look of the pale tapered limbs of a starfish clinging to a dark ocean rock. Some girls I know sneer at their madams, saying they have the hands of children, soft, useless, easily hurt, but I don't feel that way at all. I don't want my skin to grow gray and stripped and hard, for I have beautiful hands, like my father. His skin is only ever stained at the thumb and forefinger. His are the hands of a scholar.

Up, up the wide wooden stairs covered in part by a fitted carpet, dull gold with a scattering of faint green roses. At the end of the corridor is a blue-tiled water closet with porcelain fittings ("You will use the outhouse"); at the corridor's curve, four bedrooms, two on the left, two on the right. She walks into the first, a guest room. "This is called 'Birds.' You can see why." And I do. The orangey-red twin bedcovers match the custard-yellow wallpaper, and there are birds, birds, *birds* on both. They've been caught, sitting, tilting, swooping, rushing at climbing vines and each other, beaks pointing up or wide open, ready to hunt, screech, sing, dart among flowers lush with pollen. It is as though we have walked into a silent, stone-still aviary. Someone—it could only be a child—has scribbled ink onto a few of the wallpaper birds' eyes, making them blacker, sharper, so that mid-hunt, screech or song, they glare right at us.

We do not linger, she is already guiding me into the next room. "And this is 'Fontana,'" she says, pronouncing the name with a bit of drama, pointing to the back wall, which is entirely covered with a painting of what I *think* is a town square in another country. In it, a beautiful fountain gushes and very old buildings are crumbling and covered in weeds. "Isn't it hideous?" she says. "A gift from my late husband's sister, sent in the months after he died, 'to bring me comfort.' It's glued on. She suggested it go in my drawing room. Imagine! One cannot account for taste, Soraya, remember that."

"Yes, madam."

We cross the corridor, but at the first of the family bedrooms, she stops and makes a show of pulling up a pocket watch, clicking it open and checking the time. "I didn't realize the hour. We'll have to return to this room on another occasion."

Her breath has grown a little labored from all the walking and talking. She steadies herself and begins again at the fourth door. "*This* room you may enter. It is my bedroom. Come in, come in, don't hover so in the doorway."

Her bedroom is a soft sigh, a place of pale florals and spindly bedside tables. In the rest of the house, the smell of mothballs and wax polish, but here, all tangled up, the scent of dried rose petals and sprigs of fresh lavender.

Downstairs there are wide spaces between large pieces, sturdy tables, big chairs, everything covered in dark, thick brocade, the windows draped in curtains that kneel to the floor, and everywhere, everywhere, that faded maroon wallpaper. But in this room, all is delicate, slender. Even the lamps stand thin with pale bonnets and silk fringes. On each table there is something beautiful—a vase, a photograph, an ornament—and beyond, its door slightly ajar, a dressing room in shadow. Mrs. Hattingh holds herself straight, a pride pulsing off her person, and I understand that this room, unlike the others, has remained unchanged, that nothing from this room has ever had to be sold.

"Soraya?"

"Madam?"

"I see you are one for daydreaming."

"No, madam, I was just—"

"It's a great deal to absorb, I understand. Would you like to see your quarters?"

Before we leave, Mrs. Hattingh pauses for half a minute in front of a mirror as tall as she is. She tugs straight her skirt, pats at her graying reddish hair though it needs no neatening, runs her fingers back and forth over the garnet beads, neck to waist, all the while nodding at herself, smiling. Then she twists, left to right, as though taking the measure of her own trim waist. I am standing a little behind her; we are both caught in the reflection, though just a sliver of me is visible. It is only when she reaches again, as though more for pleasure than reassurance, to run her hands lightly over her bosom and torso, that I lower my gaze and stare fixedly at the carpet, at my boots peeking out from beneath my dress. I stay just like that, a faint burn on my cheeks, until she breaks from the mirror and heads for the door, saying she hopes she won't always have to chivy me along.

We cross the lawn at the back of the house. It's dry brown from a long summer, and there are more trees and fewer flowers than in the front. The garden has been pruned recently, within an inch of its life, I'd say; trees have been cut back, new soil tilled, grass sheaved. "I have a man come in every few months, and in between I will expect you to do some light weeding. As will I, my dear. I daresay there will be times we find we are working side by side. You will find me very democratic in my views." She stops for a moment to look out at her property. "A garden is a sanctuary for the soul and a responsibility for the hands."

We pass a young lemon tree, and she points at it, saying, "I planted that when my son, Master Timothy, left for the Front. In a few years it will bear fruit, and I'll be able to make the curd he loves. As a boy he'd have eaten lemon curd by the bucket if I'd let him... What's wrong? You look a little worried all of a sudden."

"Nothing, madam. Only I thought I'd be working for just you—"

"What's this, now? A confession of laziness?"

"No, madam."

"My son is in London," she says, straightening. "He went there after the war and has no intention of returning to this provincial outpost. He's very happy there. *God*. Who wouldn't be?"

"Yes, madam."

We've come up to a freestanding dwelling with two small, plain windows and a strong door. I can tell by sight that it will be freezing in winter and hot as hell in summer. Mrs. Hattingh gives a wave as though she were conjuring this all from thin air and asks if I have ever had a room of my own. I have not, I reply, thinking of my sisters at home and the other girls in my previous jobs, and at that she beams, standing taller still.

Inside, she plumps the pillows on the narrow bed, bends to smooth and pat the bleached and mended cotton covers. "The furniture in here was once in the main house." And with a final tug at a pillow's end, "You will not find me here again. I will respect your privacy."

She is expecting my thanks and I give them to her. On the floor, a round braided rug, and next to the bed, a plain table with a pale-yellow jug and bowl. There are net curtains and a small looking glass. It is a nice room and it could easily be made nicer—I imagine one of my father's protective rakams above my head and a jar of mountain daisies, fresh plucked, star bright, on the table. But there's a musty, all-wrong smell too that I can't put my finger on—it may be that the room is damp and needs an airing; it may be that an uninvited jinn has taken up residence. I resolve to burn some buchu at the first opportunity; that will take care of the problem either way.

I look over at the door's bolt: it is thick iron, firmly screwed and locks from the inside. I cannot resist touching it, testing it.

"All is in order, my dear. Fatima, the old you, was fastidious. Look around if you like! It's your room, you should get acquainted!"

There's a sweetness to her enthusiasm that is catching. I make a show of interest, opening the drawers of the dresser, touching the curtains' soft weave, looking out the small window to the lawn and its gravel pathway running between my new home and hers.

"Poor Fatima," says Mrs. Hattingh, sitting herself on the bed. "Old as the hills. She came with the house, you know. Worked here since she was a girl. Couldn't read either . . . But more devout than you, covered her face when she went into town. I'd have been lost without her, especially in those early years. She nursed me so wonderfully through the foreigners' flu, and when she caught it, I did the same for her, but she was never the same after . . . Slow to talk and such sad, sharp little breaths . . . A saint, really."

I, no saint, will soon lie where Fatima once did, slapping my face with water from the same yellow bowl, finding the dips and crevices she made in the mattress, our sighs and songs meeting somewhere in the eaves. Old Fatima would have known another girl would come to take her place, and so she's left me this gift, a strong bolt on the door.

"Well." My new employer breaks through the quiet that has formed around us. "If you've no more questions, you may go. I expect you on Monday by eight o'clock, bags in hand. No later, mind. We have much to get through."

TWO

Your Duties

Kindly bring my tea and toast up at half past seven.
   On occasion, I will take a hot breakfast downstairs.

Daily

build the fires
   do a light dust upstairs & down
   sweep the front stoep
   sweep the hallway
   take a firm brush to the rugs, paying particular attention to the ones near the fireplaces
   all household dishes must be washed before bed except the ones that need soaking overnight
   A light luncheon will do—I will discuss the menu with you on the day. I sometimes take this meal out at a friend's or the Club.

Supper is to be served every night in the dining room but for Sunday, when I will dine on my card table in the drawing room.

Weekly
wash the floors in the house, rinse down the stoep
    wash all the windows

Once a Fortnight
strip my bed of its under-sheet and launder it; leave the rest to be cleaned monthly.
    launder the clothing I have set aside: I will instruct you about which soaps to use for which garments and the temperature of the water
    air and sweep out Birds and Fontana
    scrub out the facilities
    There is a butter churner in the kitchen that you will use.
    Keep an eye—and a hand—on the garden. Some light weeding, often, should do.

Monthly
polish the silverware
    launder my remaining bedsheets and blankets
    rotate the linen in the guest room, even if there have been no guests

General
I will give you your crockery and cutlery: 1 teacup & saucer, bowl, plate, knife, fork, soupspoon. Do not, under any circumstances, use any others.

> I have an account at the general store where you will collect the eggs. (I do not keep chickens.)
>
> I have an account at the butcher. On occasion and only at my discretion, it will be put to use.
>
> Mending and repair work must be done as needed.
>
> In the spring, the curtains must come down to be washed and aired. We will choose the first hot day.

We are in the kitchen when Mrs. Hattingh reads this out loud, pausing to glance up at me, saying some words more sternly than others (*hot*, *polish*, *strip*), making sure I am paying attention. It is, I think, very like being in the schoolroom with the missionary ladies again; she speaks in their same repetitive rhythm, looks likely to take offense if I'm not paying full attention, thinks she's doing me a world of good. I am wearing the uniform she gave me; she favors the English style of a long black skirt, white blouse, high collar, but she's let me keep my head covered: *I understand your faith is important to you, Soraya,* she said.

On this first day I've chosen the brightest scarf I have, red with a thin gold thread spun through it. It's a ridiculous scarf to wear to work. I've bound it high and tight so that I gain at least four inches in height, a soft glinting crown. I'd put it on at Mrs. Hattingh's gate. If I'd worn it at home when I set out this morning, my mother would have snatched it off my head and handed me a sensible navy cotton wrap, but Mrs. Hattingh just looked amused and said, *That's very pretty*, and I realized then that she's a woman who's learned to pick her battles.

She finishes reading out the list, and I notice, with a thrum of envy, that she has exquisite penmanship; her grip is sure, her capital letters full of bold flourishes, her sentences run perfectly straight though there is no trace of pencil lines beneath them. While I can read well enough to get by, my school years were scant and so my handwriting is weak.

As she finishes, she tells me not to worry, she knows I cannot make hide nor hair of what she's written, but that she'll pin the list to the kitchen wall and read it out daily until I have it memorized. If she's missed anything, she promises, she'll just add it later: "The annual list is still to come. Let's see how these first few weeks go."

It's only then that I understand that I am still on trial.

Later and alone, I spend a long time staring at that list, going through it sentence by sentence, thinking about how my mother advised me to tell Mrs. Hattingh that I couldn't read. Some of them prize education in their servants, others resent it, she said; there's just no way of knowing where she lands. Best to keep it quiet.

I consider taking the list home on my Sunday off and showing it to Nour. Though every moment of his every day is accounted for on that awful farm—*do this, do that, here, here, here, quick, boy, I said quick, I said now, you want a klap?*—he's never made peace with being told what to do.

We've always had that in common.

It's only when I start preparing her lunch (simple fare: a poached egg with cumin roasted potatoes) that I realize that though she's arranged bunches of fresh-cut coriander and parsley in jam jars, she's not shown me where she keeps her spices.

I walk uncertainly through the house, my steps louder than I'd like. I make my way down the corridor empty of paintings, but full of a strange chill, into the wide entryway and toward the front door, where stained glass panes cast rivers of broken light on the floor.

At her drawing room door, I knock.

"Come," she says. She's seated at a desk, head down, pen in one hand, the other hand held flat up against the air so as to command my quiet, speaking as she writes: "I remain your faithful servant, Mrs. Arthur Wilmont Hattingh bracket 'Alice' bracket to jolt that fool's memory . . . almost done and *there*." She draws a line beneath her signature and looks up with a smile. "What is it?"

"Please, madam, I can't find the spices."

"I showed you earlier."

"I'm sorry, madam. I can't remember."

"In the *pantry*. The room at the end of the kitchen's passageway. If you stand at the pantry door, look to your *left*. Next to the second small table there is a cupboard with three drawers. In the third drawer you'll find the spices. *Honestly*."

"Thank you, madam."

"What are you looking for, anyway?"

"Cumin, madam."

"Oh, you'll find that in abundance—whole cumin, ground cumin, turmeric, dried chilies strung up like berries, black peppercorns, bay leaves, cinnamon scrolls, cardamom pods, cloves, even, I daresay, ones you haven't heard of, like Syrian sumac. Well?" She holds my gaze, her mouth stretching, thin lipped against large teeth. "Aren't you astonished by my knowledge?"

"Yes, madam."

"It's nothing but the result of a curious mind, Soraya. And a restless, adventuring spirit!"

"There is whole cumin, you said, madam?"

"What an anodyne little thing you are. Yes, there is whole

cumin. You may even find some potted lemons. All Fatima's doing, my dear. She kept the spice cupboard tickety-boo."

"Yes, madam. I'll go back to the kitchen now."

"Soraya."

"Madam?"

"When you came in, I was finishing a letter."

"Yes, madam."

"It was to the provost of our city's university college. I am campaigning for them to admit women. It is unthinkable that they don't. Medieval, really."

"Yes, madam."

"You will find that this is how I and some of my friends, the ones who don't *wallow*, spend our days. We make ourselves useful. Why, this week alone I have meetings scheduled about the sanitation in the District, a new sewing class for fallen girls and restocking the white workingmen's public library."

"Yes, madam."

"I'm an active woman, Soraya, my days are filled with good deeds for the world. There will be whole mornings or afternoons where you will not see me. But this does not mean that you can shirk any of your duties. This is a busy house, even if it is a quiet one."

It's evening before I have time to unpack my bag in my room. Barefoot, boots outside, I pad about, place garments in drawers, hang my second dress on the back of the door; the rakam from my father I place on a nail as high up on the wall as I can. I slip the case my mother gave me on the pillow, sit on the bed, feeling in that stillness and quiet a weight of loneliness wash over me and also the exhaustion of keeping my expressions flat, still.

One face for them, my mother had cautioned, another for us. How I had counted on going home! I put my head on the pillow. On it, in it, the scent of my mother: scrubbed fresh, sun-dried, a whiff of geranium. And it comes to me now that the thing about an obedient face is not that it doesn't work but that it works too well, that eventually it becomes the face you wear all day without even trying.

And then a flickering, something just out of sight, a billowing, a breeze, a sigh, and I realize that one of the Gray Women is here too. Of course. I should have expected as much. They're everywhere in this city, the Gray Women, stalking the streets, hanging about government buildings, frightening the horses of the rich, scaring the men who hurt them. We know them in the Quarter by their screams that mingle with the wind that blows from gorge to sea, by their shadows that hover between dusk and dark. They are neither ghost nor jinn but wholly themselves. Not jinn, because they have known flesh; not ghosts, because they do not envy the living. No, no, the Gray Women are score settlers, debt collectors, anger gatherers. The Gray Women, in their tens, hundreds even, teeming, roaming, unseen by most, covered in the thinnest coat of ash. At least one of them in every big house—usually the spirit of a servant known to the property, come either to offer counsel or to make mischief with newcomers.

I met my first Gray Woman when I was very little: she arrived in my family's home in the midst of an argument, during a hungry, hard time. *Gliding*, that's how she came, through closed doors and shut windows, right into the room I share with my sisters, and curled up at my feet, careful not to touch the others. She lay there, my first Gray Woman, watching me with big wet eyes. And there she lived, at the foot of my bed, for years and years. She had such a soft tread—just a breath at my ankles—that there were days I scarcely noticed her. Until she was angry. When she was angry, she would snap into liveliness, rise as though from a deep well, pull herself up, slip into my body, raise my temperature to almost a fever, and I would say anything to anyone. It wasn't me, I'd explain to my mother afterward, it was one of the Gray Women.

This Gray Woman is shimmering about my new room, retracing Mrs. Hattingh's steps, now leaning over the bed, now standing by the window. She's not taken shape just yet—that, I know from past experience, may take a little while, but it will happen. For now, she's a feeling, a knowingness.

Who *is* she? It could only be old Fatima.

I may as well acknowledge her. Be respectful. Get on her good side. I sit up. "Greetings, Auntie," I say out loud, but she's already left. Drifted back to the house probably, if that's where her loyalties lie. Or even if they don't.

I lie down again, grateful to finally be alone, realizing that I'd forgotten to pack the buchu. God, I think, covering my eyes with my hand. Comes with the house indeed.

Mrs. Hattingh likes her routine just so. I am up at five thirty to build two fires, in the kitchen and in the drawing room. Mrs. Hattingh tells me this is her one extravagance, to have fires even in the warm season, for she is "susceptible to chills" and 23 Heron Place has "cold bones."

I take her a tray at seven thirty.

"I'm up early, always early," she says cheerily, by way of greeting. "If there is one thing I cannot abide, it's a layabout."

On the tray, a pot of tea, two slices of toast propped up in the silver rack, a small round of butter and a serving of my mother's golden kumquat jam. "This is splendid, Soraya!" she says the first time she tastes it, and promises to tell all her friends to order a batch.

Each morning I remind myself that I am very lucky to have this position, that cleaning and cooking for one unusually kind woman is any maid's dream. But the work is *dull*, endlessly dull. I could sleepwalk through a day here, I think during that first week, and as long as I'm not handling something hot and heavy, I probably wouldn't need to wake up. There are ways, though—there are always ways—to slip past the boredom, disappear, dissolve, let the edges of this world soften and a new, silvery one form.

When I was a girl, I would gather up the other children in the Quarter, walk us up to the top of the hill that overlooks our city and command them to stand in a circle around me. *Moon to star*, I would say, *moon to star*. I'd tell them to *Be quiet*. And then, *Listen*. All around us, the thrum and menace of mountain life: a rustle in the brush, the hum of insects, the scuttle of something rock to rock.

And into their quiet I would tell stories, ones that had come to me in a dream or on a day of dissolving while washing, weeding or walking, stories that I swore to the children were real.

In the Quarter, we have a story about a man who appears only at dusk, as the day stretches into night. Always on horseback, he is dressed in the finest silk robes, his animal decorated with shining jewels. He holds a flute to his mouth and plays a song so beautiful that it draws the children from their homes, and they follow him, as if in a dream, toward the mountain and into the caves.

I became like that man. All I had to do was tell the other children I was going up the hill and they would trail after me, waiting for a story.

I would start with a lowered voice: *If a prayer begins by acknowledging God and the Devil, a story should begin by acknowledging Good and Evil, and this is a story about Good and Evil. A story about the Cape. Names and addresses have been changed to protect reputations.*

One day I pushed too far, took the measure of them and misjudged, told a story that sent their spines ashiver and changed everything for me. I said to them, "This is not a story for children. If you fear the dark, you must not listen. If you don't like to wash your face (and shame on you if you don't), if you fight your mother when she makes you take abdas, then this is not a story for you. Because this story has it all. This is a story about a woman who lives in the water, and the water around her is always dark, not just because she wears only and every day a black abaya (ragged at the hem, the edges nibbled by fish; torn down the front from when she fought a shark by herself and won!). Dark not just because of her dress, but dark because every day she seeps (exactly, precisely) ninety-nine drops of blood. The blood is a cloud around her, blurring her robe as she moves in and between the sway and give of the seaweed. Though she has legs, her toes are so close together people mistake her feet for fins.

"Her blood is not red but ink black, because she is not really alive, not like you or me, you see. Not quite like us. She's a thing between us and the dead (a brave thing! a powerful thing!). She is the blood in the water, the water between the worlds. Her dark blood is the magic that keeps her safe.

"It is the blood that warns all others, be they fish or foe, plant or ship, to stay back!"

I stopped to look at each and every one of them, was satisfied when I saw one child crying with fright and went on only when Nour, grinning on the side, gave a nod.

"Now listen," I continued. "*Listen*," I said.

The children moved in closer.

"Once, a sailor feeling the heat of the high midday sun (just like this one) dove off his ship's hull into the deep give of the blue ocean. He was famous for holding his breath for minutes at a time. *Minutes*. Can you imagine?

"Down, down, down in the deep, he sees the seawoman in among the plants and rocks, sees her robe move around her like another self, and on top of the robe, a cloud of something. Beneath the robe, he thinks he glimpses her form—beautiful and free like a song he once knew.

"Everything inside him grows tight. He does not know, could not know, that the cloud that surrounds her is blood. Instead, he thinks, It's ink. *Ink*.

"So, he tells himself, she is one of those ocean creatures that bleeds ink.

"And then says out loud (though who can hear him? Only the gulls and the waves), 'I have not had a woman in so long, and I've run out of ink. Now, I can have both. I will capture her and drag her to my ship. I will collect the ink and write all about my travels.'

"He swims toward her waving his knife, and she smiles. He lowers his knife— Just look at that welcome, he thinks. She opens her arms, her robes flowing soft and sure with the tide, and he pushes toward her, ready to grab her hair, tug her to the surface, push the knife into her side if he must.

"He moves closer, still holding his breath, and she reaches out, grabs him close, and he sees that she has grown the extra arms of a fearsome octopus, the tips of her now forty fingers sucking on his skin.

"At first, he is in ecstasy, but then fear takes hold and he begins to struggle, shouting, 'Let me go!' But no sound comes from his mouth. Instead, the water takes his words and sends them far away. With seven hands she clasps him to her breast, and with the eighth she takes up the hem of her robe and washes his face. She washes, washes, washes, and then at last when she is satisfied that he is just as clean as can be, she lets him go. He floats back up to the surface, nose in the air, the skin stripped from his face.

"He was no longer a man," I said, slamming one hand into the other. "He was a warning."

Two more of the children began to cry. The rest of us bade the loudest one to be quiet, but she turned tail and ran down the hill, and we chased after her, past the mosque, left at the open field, toward the street where the three trees were in bloom—lemon, hibiscus, loquat—one step, two steps, onto her stoep, and she ran directly into her mother's arms, stupid, stupid, tjanking up a storm. Because of *her*, word spread up and down our streets that I spun wicked tales that set children's dreams on fire, invited the jinn to dine at our tables, brought too much or too little rain, drove the heat causing the soaps to melt, the meat to poison, the milk to spoil; that my parents should wash my mouth with lye, give me a good thrashing, mantra me out, sacrifice a sheep as penance if it wasn't so expensive. My parents let the talk swirl and hum about them, and once everyone in the Quarter had had their say, once they'd shared their longed-for punishment-cures, my father shut our front door. My mother spoke to him in a low, hushed voice about how I seemed to slip sometimes between this world and the next, that she knew, she *knew*, that the veil between the realms was thin for me, nothing, a breath, an onion skin, a spider's thread; that when I wasn't dreaming, I seemed incapable of getting through the simplest task from start to end, startled by this or that—a wagon passing by, a child in the street, a bird calling into the night—and it was strange, didn't my father see that it was *strange*, and perhaps our child is *strange*, she went on, and then, as though already arguing angrily with someone who had dared to say that her child was strange, she'd just tell them where to go and which way to look, but that even so, it worried her, *worried* her, because I had to be of this world to make my way through it, I couldn't be wandering between realms willy-nilly, I needed my wits about me, feet on *this* earth, eyes on *this* fire.

He said very little in response, my father, just stole into his back room to finish drawing a prayer he'd been working on all week, and my mother's shoulders drooped. I watched as she hunched, head in hands, over the kitchen table, then roused herself, calling for me. The time for storytelling, she said, was over and the time for work had begun. And no nonsense about the Gray Women either. She handed me a barrel of sopping sheets and a slab of soap and said, "Scrub. Scrub these sheets clean and be glad I'm not scrubbing out your mouth."

The next week, she sent me out to service.

THREE

In the first week here, I learn how the light moves from room to room. In the morning the front of the house gets the full blinding force of the Cape sun; it pierces through thick curtains, sending the night's dust into a twirling dance. From here, I can see the harbor, and that's when I long most for home. The Quarter, though up a hill and a distance from the ocean, feels somehow very close to it. And if you climb the hill till you're standing right by the cannon, the one that strikes each midday (*A weapon for a clock,* my father says, *these people, telling time by a gun*), you will see to your right the mountain cut against the sky, and to your left, in a sweep below, the edge of the city and the sea that brought us here.

I work my way from these windows, past the ones in the hallway, to the back where the kitchen is. Mornings in the kitchen are dim, cool. The ceiling is low, and when the garden trees cast their leaf-light on wooden floors and white stone walls, I feel as though I am in a forest.

On the first day, cloth in one hand, broom in another, I'd stood in the vast drawing room, bewildered. Where to clean first? I almost called out to old Fatima for advice, but if she *is* the Gray Woman, she's not yet returned, and heaven knows, those women are not ones to be summoned.

Alone I worked out that if I really wanted to see what's what and have it come up shining, I had best start at the front of the house in the morning and make my way to the back in the afternoon. Mrs. Hattingh does the opposite: as the day unfolds, she moves away from the sun, as though she's trying to stay always in the twilight.

In those first days I learned that the staircase creaks as the beams of the house stretch, and though I took a fright the first few times—*What was that? Who was that? Fatima? Someone else?*—I realized quickly that it wasn't a roaming spirit, just the house making its own noises, maybe even telling me it was happy having me traipse up and down. *More life,* I thought I heard the house sing, *more life*.

I learned too that in a house this big (bigger even than the Edenburgs'), with its high ceilings, long corridors and wide entryways, that the smells of people—what we eat, need, burn, make—all disappear into nothing. In the Quarter, smells *stay*. There's the smell in our houses of incense burning both now and fifty years ago, of a thousand meals past and the ones bubbling on stoves this minute. Sticking to every wall, woven into every curtain, the reek of chopped onions and pressed garlic, the trace of scattered methi, diced chilies, dried bay leaves; of spices—whole, roasted, ground, cast in hot oil—and of meat braising, bones boiling, fat spitting, broth cooking, sugar burning, rose water steaming, tea brewing, mint leaves just torn, ginger beer just poured. It's the smell of more in good times and of keeping an eye in lean ones. In our house, also, the whiff of my mother's soaps, the sweet jasmine my father planted at the front gate, the sticky heat of my and my sisters' sweat, the rush of the tides my brother brings back with him from a day at the beach and the fish he carries, still on the hook, sea fresh, glassy-eyed, salt crusted, scales shining.

None of that at Heron Place.

But small house, big house, smells or no smells, this much is the same: that in this city you will come to know a person by two things: what's inside their house, and the house's way with the wind. At Heron Place the wind comes at night, first at a creep, then a roar. It curls around the bend, then moves at ocean force down the street, churning up mountain dust that makes for daytime grime. And Mrs. Hattingh's remaining ornaments and furniture—*All from my family or travels, my dear*—have a talent for trapping dust. Among the pieces, a full-bellied laughing stone man with fat child cheeks that she keeps at the front door—*Our household god. I like to scandalize the parish priest, Soraya, I can't bear small-mindedness*—an ivory elephant—*Wait until I tell you about its provenance*—engraved side tables and vases thick with grapes and golden cherubs—*My grandmother's, I suppose I must hang on to them*—intricate wooden screens with woven reed windows—*Now these are quite special; they date back to when the settlers first arrived here, brought, I believe, on the same ship as the people who made them! Your people, Soraya. Wonderful craftsmen. You should be very proud.* Brass- and silver-framed photographs crowd the top of the piano—*This, my wedding. My veil was woven by girls at a lace school for the blind. This is Master Timothy at his christening, and here he is in his school uniform; look at those little socks! And those are my parents. Do be careful with all of these, they are irreplaceable.* So many porcelain figurines: a woman dancing, a shepherdess tending a sheep, a boy strumming a harp. Persian carpets that she walks on without removing her shoes. Lace doilies on sofas—*Do you crochet, my dear? Fatima was a dab hand at it. No? Pity. We'll soon remedy that. It's a good skill, and I'm sure you have your people's nimble fingers.*

Each thing, she vows, is precious to her.

But the dust, I want to say.

The dust, the dust, the *dust*.

Daily dust.

Dust to dust.

Straight off the mountain, brought in by the wind, looking for somewhere to land.

And each day, a new fight, because Mrs. Hattingh hates dust as much as she loves her stone god, her shepherdess, her harpist, her screens. She hates dust so much that she will sometimes, even after I've cleaned, go back to a table, cloth in hand, and give it another wipe, or take a small toothpick to clean out the grit in an ornament's crevice. She complains about the dust more than she complains about anything else, so much so that I wonder why she stays in this house on the mountain's slope, where the wind's endless song will always mean a fine sheen of dirt and an unsettled mind.

One morning I learn that the dust comes in (and in and *in*) because there are gaps where some of the sash windows close. The wood is old and worn away, the brass greenish, marks of wind and sea-salt air. Mrs. Hattingh must know about it because someone (it could only be her) has stuffed a recent newspaper into the small openings and then arranged the curtains to conceal it. It looks unsightly. Poor. I could just keep adding newspaper, but instead I make a point of telling her that the windows need repairing. I don't say out loud how terrible it looks; I just make my eyes very wide as though I can't quite believe what I am seeing. I tell her that my uncle is a joiner, and he could do the job, that he does the governor's house too. She stands there, staring at the gaps, before answering, "Yes, yes, of course. I will need to consult with my son; he may have a recommendation of his own and that will take a while. Letters to London take an age. But he likes to be kept abreast of any matters relating to the house. Do remind me, my dear."

Among all her precious things, it is the elephant that demands the most careful cleaning. Carved from ivory, it is at least a foot tall and Mrs. Hattingh's pride. It lives in her drawing room, brought here by her father's father from his time in India—*Such a beautiful country, Soraya, such interesting people, very spiritual, but fighters too. They can be very fierce, even when unprovoked. An elephant carved from ivory—really, it's a terribly clever idea.*

I agree. It is terribly terrible.

Whenever I touch it, I can't help but think that it is the same as someone carving a small likeness of a man from his very own leg bone.

I clean every part of it: the tiny toenails, the folds and ridges of the curved trunk, the eyes spread wide and flat on the head, ears midflap, tuning in, wary, alert to a distant danger. The longer I hold it, the more the ivory warms against my hot hands. What is it my father always says? *Something that lived once can stay living: trees milled into paper, a bird's feather made into a quill, sheep's hair woven into wool.*

Things go on, he insists always, *even in death.*

My father also says that there are two types of makers: the one who loves and the one who is empty. If you love, what you make will seem to move even in stillness. If you give your work your life's breath, it will keep something of you even when it is in the world without you. But if you are empty, if you don't share your breath, it is possible that what you make will be perfect, but there will be nothing inside of it, and more, nothing will come out of it. Each time I look at this elephant I come to understand a little more about how its maker loved it. I think about him, the carver, being handed the hacked-off tusk, blood on the bone, flesh still clinging to it; how he must have cleaned it, then gotten to work, trying to bring the creature back to itself.

But the ivory animal is nothing compared with what I see in Mrs. Hattingh's bedroom.

I'm in her room, kneeling in front of the fireplace, about to polish the floral tiles and scrape the ash from the grate, when I feel a pair of eyes on me. I look up, and sure enough someone is there, right there, on the wall above the mantelpiece. My throat closes, my eyes flare, my head snaps to the side, because, I think, it *can't* be what it seems to be. I drop the brass shovel and jump to my feet, not minding how the ash flies out before me. My tongue goes from moist to bone-dry, and with the quickness of a fire, a feeling of being drawn out of my body, of floating up, takes me over.

The eyes belong to the girl in a painting hanging above the fireplace. Long necked, her skin the color of roasted coriander seeds, eyes dark, mouth parted just a little as I do before I ask a question, a scarf draped lightly over her head and her glance cool, just off to the side, mocking, staring at me from under her lashes.

It's *me*, I think. A painting of *me*. Bold as you please, hanging in the old woman's room. How did I come to be here? And why didn't I see it on the first day?

I step back, the fire brush still in my hand, my skirt awash with ash, my mind ascramble. But the longer I look, the more I realize that it is not quite me, not really, more as though the painter once saw me, then painted what he remembered.

"I see you admiring my Rosa." Mrs. Hattingh is at the doorway. "I don't think she was up when you interviewed?"

I shake my head.

"No, you're right. She was in my dressing room. She's terribly heavy but I do like to move her around . . . I think she enjoys it too. Change of scenery. Would you look at the dust on that frame? Devilishly difficult, these old gilt things. Thank goodness you're here to help with that now. She's lovely, isn't she, my Rosa? A gift from the previous owners of Heron Place, so she's been here for *donkey's* years. Came with the house. Worth a small fortune now apparently. And from your neighborhood, I'm told, but ever so long ago. You know, the moment I saw you, I was struck by your likeness to her."

I reply that I thought she looked familiar, even as I fight a sudden wildness to reach up, snatch Rosa off the wall and run, *run*, taking us both home.

"My husband and I once collected all sorts of paintings about the Cape, and Rosa gave us our start. He found so much about this little city fascinating . . . You are taken with her. I can tell." Mrs. Hattingh walks over to stand by my side and, as we gaze up at Rosa together, says, "Mind, when you dust the frame, you don't touch her face."

She sits on the very edge of her bed and gestures at me to get back to work, talking while I scrape away at the soot lodged deep and blackened in the fireplace's grooves.

"When I was a girl in England, I loved to paint. My governess would lay out the most marvelous arrangements—flowers, fruit, paisley silk, brass ornaments from the Orient—mostly from my grandfather's travels. I'd spend hours with my oils, my watercolors. I was quite good . . . My governess said I had some talent. She'd bring me wonderful books full of prints of famous paintings, and once, we went down to London and spent a blissful day together at the National Gallery. It was heavenly, and I told myself as soon as I was out, I'd run away to Paris—City of Light!—live in a little attic, take up smoking and paint all day. Imagine! Of course, I stopped that foolishness when I got married. Mr. Hattingh had an absolute fit one day early in our marriage, in the first months I was here; I was supposed to have spent the morning hiring a new cook, and instead, he found me all adream and drawing flowers in the garden. He was *livid*. There was no new cook, not a meal to be found, and a young wife with charcoal-covered hands. He threw out my brushes and paper and forbade me from painting ever again." She gives a little laugh. "Quite right too, I suppose."

I turn over my own hands, now coated in ash, and feel rising between us a small being, dark as the ocean at night, heavy, formless, the sum of her sadness, more of what my mother would call foolishness. She must feel it too, or something like it, because she's quick to add, "Don't look so glum, my dear! Instead, he promised I could buy all the paintings I liked. And I did! Mr. Hattingh was a good deal older than me and so he had rather different tastes; he adored traditional paintings—horses, ships, landscapes—but I love portraits. *Faces.* Done in the newer style, vivid colors, *oomph*, a loose brush and a canny eye. There was a time when the whole of the downstairs corridor was just lined with faces, mostly of your people, Soraya. Men, women and children in rich oils and pastels, some in rags, some in silks, most of them pensive or sad, and my late husband would say, 'Do we *have* to have these miserable blacks staring at us all day?'"

She giggles remembering her husband's little joke, and I understand, finally, the feeling of being watched as I passed through that corridor, face after face, still there, still trapped, still looking.

"In the end, the paintings served us well. Mr. Hattingh died when Master Timothy was just fourteen—not cut down in his prime, but certainly sooner than I'd have expected. Tuberculosis, poor man. It's a wretched, painful end, my dear. I sold all the paintings—had to! Except this one. She's my company, Rosa. You can tell the artist was a little bit in love with her, with Rosa, don't you think?"

She doesn't wait for my reply, just gets up and says with a sigh before she drifts off, "Do sweep up all the ashes, won't you?"

Alone, I look at the painting. And she, Rosa, looks back at me from the corner of her eye.

In love with her?

"In love with you?" I ask Rosa.

Rosa doesn't budge, just keeps her ever cool, sidelong glance. Later, in the quiet of this room, as I work a wet cloth over my soot-covered hands, she whispers to me about the months spent in the chair, the coldness of the room, the chiffon clutched around her because the artist wanted to see her flesh even if he didn't paint it, how a prayer still hangs on a gold chain about her neck, swinging out of the frame.

In love with me. She laughs, her voice suddenly rising from rasp to bark.

I am only half frightened by this, because in this city, none of us really knows the truth of the ground we stand upon or the things we own. Even in the Quarter, where our men pray as they build our homes, we do not always know what lives within the walls, what sits deep in the soil or what nightly sings in the grass and trees. I know this to be true because there are times when the dead who visit in the Quarter are not familiar to us; they are from a time before. They walk into our homes and look around, bewildered. One such pair, a father and his small daughter, came right into our front room and stood there in their leather coverings and deerskin boots. The father held up a necklace, a string of pretty seashells, that had been smashed beyond repair. He spoke a tongue none of us understood and used his hands to tell us it was *the New People, the sailors*, who shattered it. He looked down at the broken jewelry and then at us, as if to say, *Who would do such a thing? Who would do such a thing?* Days went by and the spirit visitors would not leave our house, and so my mother walked them across town to the District, where old Mina the soothsayer lived. She told my mother she'd done the right thing, bringing them to her, and then went on to talk the father and daughter over from this world to the next. They left the necklace with her as thanks.

Rosa's gone quiet. She looks a little panicked. Maybe she's worried she's scared me off.

"It's all right," I tell her as I finish up the grate and pack away my brushes. "You can talk to me. I am not afraid."

FOUR

Tuesday mornings at Heron Place have an extra pulse to them because it is the day the postman makes his rounds and Mrs. Hattingh may hear from her London son. He writes monthly, she tells me, but the post—*the post in this country*—is often delayed, uneven, sometimes a letter doesn't come for two months, sometimes three letters come at once. Still, she waits each week at the gate, aflutter, aflutter, for the man to arrive. Today, on my third Tuesday here, the sun climbs, an unseasonal heat rises, gathers, turns in on itself, and she is forced to remove her straw hat and use it as a fan. I watch her from the drawing room window; even at this distance I can see her body is taut and she jolts at every sound—wagon creak, birdsong, wasp rage, church bells. When the postman rounds the corner she opens the gate, springs toward him, meets him in the street. He always seems to understand her urgency, to know it well, and today he is smiling, holding a letter out from several paces away. They speak for a few moments, then she turns, taking the envelope to her breast before using a handkerchief to dab at her sweat-drenched face.

She walks up the pathway toward the house, already opening the letter, reading it. I jump back from the window and run to the kitchen to fetch her a glass of cool water. My mother has taught me that doing things for them *before* they ask is the quickest way to gain their favor, and sure enough, she smiles widely when I bring the water out to her.

"Thank you, Soraya, ten steps ahead I see."

"It's so hot today, madam. A person will sweat out there."

"Horses sweat, Soraya. Men perspire. And ladies gently glow."

"Yes, madam."

"My son has sent a little sum along with his letter from London. Dear boy, so like him, he makes every effort to ease my burdens."

She's relieved, that's clear; the money means she'll be able to settle all accounts—from butcher to milkman, milkman to seamstress—and stop hiding when they knock, which they've already done a few times since I've been here. This seems a good moment to ask her if I could possibly go home before the next fortnight's end. I have been missing my family so much, I tell her, and I need be gone only for a few hours. I remind her how very close by the Quarter is.

Mrs. Hattingh doesn't answer me; instead, she says she'll take her luncheon a little later to give me a chance to prepare it, as there's a quantity of work to be done first. Later, she calls me to her drawing room and shares with obvious happiness, as though I am more friend than maid, that her son writes that he is planning to visit. He's not given a specific date, but soon: two, three months at most. "We have much to look forward to. But more, we have much to plan, to make ready. To work! To work!"

I do not ask about an early visit home again.

The next day, the preparations for her son's visit begin. Apparently, the entire house has to be scrubbed clean months before he arrives, and this, I quickly realize, means that she will be home more than usual. The poor, the suffering, the girls eager to gain entrance to university, will all have to wait. She instructs me to make a start by taking out the table linen stored in the dining room cupboards—*Each and every cloth must be aired, soaked, washed, possibly bleached, Soraya, who can say?* I pull out tablecloths, runners, place mats, fluff them out and immediately begin to sneeze. So much dust. When last had Fatima done this? Mrs. Hattingh has dining cloths in every style—lace, linen, cotton, light calico, embroidered, crocheted, fancy, plain, cream, white, sometimes color—and as I pull out this one, then that one, I find, tucked between napkins, a heavy, thick silver frame and, in it, a photograph of a young man, a pilot. This must be Master Timothy. Whoever he is, he stands posed with one hand in his pocket, arm jutting out like the wing of a sparrow. Across the other arm, a draped leather jacket, flying goggles around his neck. Behind him is a grounded airplane that gives me, even in stillness, a feeling of terror, of swooping wonder. There's a softness to his eyes I haven't seen very often in men like him. A dreamy fellow, I think, and take the cloth to wipe down the dusty glass, handling him with extra care, and that's just how Mrs. Hattingh finds us: me holding him, us staring at each other.

"What are you doing?"

It's as though she grows wings, for she flies from the doorway to where I am standing and snatches the frame from my hands. She holds it tight against her person, then gives a soft laugh and says she can't think what came over her.

"It's my son," she says without my asking, turning the frame toward me. "I'd forgotten he was in there."

Smiling, she places his picture on top of the piano with the rest of the photographs.

"Shall I tell you something very foolish? I packed this away as soon as it was framed. Stuffed it in that drawer. I had this idea that it was bad luck to have it out while the war was on—Timothy dressed up and ready for danger. It felt . . . not *boastful*, but as though I were tempting fate. And you know, I wasn't entirely wrong. Every mother I know who had her son's pictures out—many of them friends—not one of their boys survived. Mrs. Lockday, who was here last week, had four sons, *four*, mind you, and she lost every one of them. I went to a Lockday funeral every season for an entire year, and even now, when I see her near a vase of flowers, I can't help but think of her standing by the arrangements next to their caskets. Dreadful. Do you know what she did?"

I shake my head. Mrs. Hattingh presses on.

"She went to a woman, someone who can see the dead, *talks* to them, something of that sort. She wanted to . . . *make contact* with her sons. You look shocked, my dear. I thought your people knew all about this sort of thing."

Though the day is summer warm, a coldness floods me. It's not what her friend did. Any of the women in the Quarter might have done the same. It's the turn in Mrs. Hattingh's tone, mocking, sly, a small smile as though she is inviting me to laugh in disbelief alongside her.

"Ah, now your shock has turned to disapproval. Well, I can only tell you what she told me, that she *spoke* with one of her boys. Actually spoke to him. The youngest one, Felix. Sweetest boy. He 'came through,' as the seer described it." Her face changes again, and she leans toward me, speaks almost in a whisper. "And *then* she said—and this I could scarcely believe—that if the bishop disapproved, he could go to hell. She told me this woman, this soothsayer, had given her more comfort in a few minutes than the Church had given her in all the years since Ypres." Mrs. Hattingh draws back, mouth twitching. "Apparently, the woman said things like, 'He has brown eyes, is neither short nor tall,' that he was at 'rest,' so really, a lot of nonsense, but it seemed to give her some peace. Imagine! Having to go to those lengths to settle your own heart. Awful."

But Mrs. Lockday, Mrs. Hattingh went on, had *nothing* on another one of her friends, Mrs. Ramsay. *She* lost her boy too, but instead of going into proper mourning, she announced that she was going to give talks about the war. "She booked the Rotary Hall through the women's club, saying she was going to do a presentation about the boys, so *naturally* we went to support her. Even the parish priest came. We all went thinking we'd listen to her read some letters, hear a few songs, send round the collection jar . . . But it was nothing of the sort. In fact, it was ghastly. She started off, not with a prayer, but a poem, with none of the appropriate patriotic feeling. And *then*—I've still no notion of how she procured them—*then* came the photographs." Ditches, Mrs. Hattingh went on, lined with boys with rotting boots and bone-thin dogs. Old men saluting commanding officers young enough to be their sons. Boys getting care packages—at least *that* was decent. Rifles and clear skies, fields and hospital tents, and then, with no warning, *none whatsoever*, empty canisters, gassy fog, barbed wire, burned and twisted trees, boys bandaged up on stretchers, and oh, it was a dreadful business. No one could bear it. Mrs. Ramsay talked very fast and said the most terrible things, horrible details about shrapnel and blood and operations without morphine or even some strong drink to ease the pain, and it was the detail, the *detail*, that was so difficult. Finally, even Father Anselm had had enough, told her he needed to have *a word* and then led her out. "He asked her to stop because it wasn't good for morale. And she did. She stopped talking about most things. She went from being someone who never stopped speaking to someone who was quiet as a mouse in the blink of an eye."

It's as though having the photograph out has turned her tongue even looser, because in the days that follow all she can talk about is Timothy. (*Master Timothy*, she says when she remembers, as though I might slip up when we meet. Sometimes, drawing herself up, *Lieutenant Hattingh*.) Master Timothy was one of the first boys in the colony to volunteer; he needed no pamphlets or coaxing or shaming, he was just naturally courageous, inclined to do the right thing. He'd stood up to bullies since he was a boy, even to his father before he died (*Really, Soraya, Mr. Hattingh, bless him, had the fiercest temper*), and his headmaster—why wouldn't he take on the Hun? He was also a whiz at flying—just took to the skies. A Knight of the Sky. *The pilots were special, Soraya, different from the trench boys. You needed courage in spades and the brains to match to become one.* Master Timothy shot down his fair number of Germans, there's even a medal! It's in her room, if I'd like to have a look? Dear boy, he sent it down for her to keep. Oh yes, a war hero. But he didn't escape entirely unscathed. Alas! He sustained a few injuries—minor (he complains, even today, of aches and things, especially in the winter months)—but alive, *alive*. Think of the others. Think of their fates in the trenches. Boys she knew, boys who were frequent guests in her house. Timothy's friends. It still feels nearly impossible to face their mothers. That's why she pays such short calls, doesn't invite them around much, always makes sure that when they *do* see each other, it's *tied* to something, preferably good works, something that can take them *outside* of themselves. Better this way. Perhaps Timothy can't face them either, because he's been working in London ever since the war ended.

She sighs sadly, then says, her brows knitting together, *Mad luck, Soraya, that's what surviving a war is, mad luck*. He was first in France, then transferred to the Megiddo in Palestine, where things were not as bad. Hot as Hades there, stuck in the desert, surrounded by strangers and, worse, locals, but still, better lonely and alive than dead with your companions. She wishes she had a more recent likeness of him, but he hasn't sent one over. She's worried he may be embarrassed about a little twitch he says he's developed, but she's sure it will pass in no time.

He's been promising a visit for so long, but now is the first time he can come out. You see, he's reading law at university *alongside* his solicitor's clerkship, and it takes *time* to settle into a job there, it's not like here where you just walk into something because someone knew your father or they've taken a shine to you, and anyway, he writes as much and as often as he is able. He's written again, this time with a date—he'll be here by September 16! Or the 23rd if the boat runs late. Not as soon as she'd like, but he plans to stay through Christmas, so we best get the house spick-and-span. She *may* even have to hire someone else for when he is here. A manservant, someone who can do a bit of valeting, some heavy lifting.

Do I know of anyone? He's mentioned—and here she betrays the first trace of worry I've seen when she speaks about any of this—that he needs a little more help these days. Just getting his coat on, that sort of thing.

Oh, he writes often, her son. Often enough. Not so often that he replies to every one of *her* letters—she laughs at this and says then that no son on earth has ever written to his mother as much as she'd like, and her boy is no exception. But when the letters do come! My! They are just jam-packed with news. London, she tells me, is back on its feet and all manner of new fashions are about. It wouldn't surprise her, she says, following me outside to the washing line, if he had a young lady over there and wasn't quite ready to tell his dear mama about her. At any rate, it makes sense that he's staying there for now, after all; it's his homeland, even if he was born here. *She* was born in a place called Devon, but she will not go back, she will never go back, she will not leave this house. If she leaves the house, how will she make sure that his room is ready for him when he returns? She'd had him late, quite late—nearly thirty!—after a string of *disappointments*, but that made them all the closer. For instance, she can sense, she says, adjusting one of the clothespins I've just set, even from *this* distance, that he's not invited her because he knows how long journeys tire her. Besides, there's something lovely about being *home* to welcome him back. No, no, she won't go to London until she's asked, she doesn't want to crowd him. So many mothers do that, and it's the quickest way to lose your son. *Remember that, Soraya, when you have a son—though I do hope that's many years away! Don't* hover. *They hate that.*

I have sorted, scrubbed, bleached and dried the linen by the time she finishes talking. If she had one more son to speak of, I could probably have finished the whole of the downstairs. Two more, this house would be sheening.

The room she is staying home to take care of, to make ready, is the same one she told me not to enter on the day of my interview. I've been in since—it's been added to the weekly to-do list—and it is exactly as he left it four years ago; nothing there has been sold or stripped. His school uniform is in the wardrobe, his shoes in a row, polished. Even the model biplane still hangs from the ceiling, and when the wind blows it makes circles and circles. She seldom goes into this room and then only for a moment or two, but weekly I must sweep the floors, wipe down the books, dust the battalions of tiny toy soldiers. It's quick work, but I take my time because I know she won't disturb me in here. When she passes this room, she usually quickens her pace. Just once, I saw her stop. She put a hand on the doorknob and leaned her forehead against the door. She stayed there for a long moment like a doctor waiting, listening for a breath. I could tell then how much she misses him, how lonely she is, and I wondered how any child could treat his mother with such coldness. What had she done to deserve this? She shrank when she heard me behind her and kept her face turned to the door. I knew that if I'd gone to her, if I'd touched her shoulder, even lightly, she would have cried and I would have had to hold her, soothe her, as Fatima probably did. But I do not have the patience for or interest in Mrs. Hattingh's tears. In the same way that she wants me to be one thing, a servant, no more, I want her to be one thing. Let us stay this way. I will be the silent figure in her house, listener to her endless chatter; I will bring her tea and turn down the covers. This is enough. This is enough.

* * *

After days of Master Timothy talk, she stops. She even looks a little abashed as I bring in her tray at teatime, as though she knows she's spoken too much and too long about her son. She says, "But I know next to nothing about your family, Soraya. You must tell me *everything*."

The questions begin.

I tell her only what I can stand to give:

"Yes, madam, Mother and Father are still alive . . . There are four of us children, three girls—myself, Lia and Alma—and a boy, Kashif . . . Yes, madam, a small family for our people . . . I *am* engaged, madam, yes. His name is Nour . . . No, madam, he no longer lives in town. Jobs are scarce. He found work some months ago on a farm just outside the city . . . No, madam, he does not go home every fortnight, he is given one Sunday off a month; sometimes he comes home, sometimes he doesn't. It's hours of travel both ways."

She stiffens when I say this and riffles around her desk for a pamphlet. She waves it toward me: "Goodness, Soraya, are you aware of the conditions farm laborers face? I hope Nour isn't subject to any beastliness."

I thank her for her concern.

"You know, I am surprised to learn you are marrying a farm laborer. You can't read or write, but still, you seem to be a girl of some refinement. I cast no aspersions when I say this, but I had hoped for better for you."

It is all I can do not to scream that there would be nothing amiss if this were Nour's only work, but in fact she's partly right, because he is reaching toward something different, better; the brightest boy in our people's school, he is going to be a teacher but needs to set some money aside for himself and his parents before he takes to years of study. He began work on the farm a little before I started at

Heron Place, and it is backbreaking and difficult, but he is uncomplaining. I tell her a little of this, and as I do, she claps her hands, eyes shining, saying, "But this is so wonderful! Who set him on this path?"

"The missionaries, madam, at the school for boys."

"Admirable souls!"

"Yes, madam."

"A teacher-to-be. There are such dignified examples among your people, Soraya, working away to uplift your race. And to think Nour may be one of them."

I wish I hadn't told her about any of it.

I busy myself with the tray, but her questions continue rapid-fire, and I am obliged to keep answering them.

"Yes, madam, we want to marry in a few years."

"Goodness, I hope you're not planning to abandon me after that, Soraya."

"No, madam."

"And whatever else, no babies for the first year. At least."

I flinch but say nothing and she forges on.

"Yes, madam, we have always lived in the Quarter."

"The *Quarter*," she echoes in a hushed voice filled with wonder, as though I am speaking about the moon, and then, "Shall I tell you something? I knew a settler woman who turned to your faith. *Converted*. She was so taken with your people's ways she became one of you."

I arrange my face to show the surprise I know she wants to see, but really, I am not astonished. There was a time, not so long ago, when these sorts of women developed a hankering for our way. Some of them were famous for it; they said the sacred words and then wrote books about their new selves, and everyone from here all the way to London Town made a big fuss over them, as if believing in God were something special instead of the most ordinary thing in the world. My father's father helped one of these women with her conversion, and when I asked him about it, he said it was as though she had awoken from a deep slumber and had found the truth, but my mother said that was nonsense, that it was because her husband was a violent drunk and their faith let him drink—they even made it a part of their holy rituals—and that her being like us was one way to stop the drink at the door. It was an awful lot of trouble, my mother declared, to go through for a bottle of wine.

I'm taking a damp cloth to the table when I realize Mrs. Hattingh is still speaking. She repeats herself, loudly, rapping her knuckles on the table with each word.

"I *said*, do you know if anyone in your family was once a slave?"

I do not pause in my wiping. After a long moment I say, "I don't know. My grandmother may have been as a girl. We were told never to ask her."

Another question, this time in a hair above a whisper.

I reply, my voice firm: "No, madam, the thought of it doesn't make me sad."

Sadness, I want to tell her, crossly, is for the here and now. It is for broken lips and stained clothing and dry bread borrowed for supper and working on a farm though you are the brightest boy in the school. To go looking for sadness, to go digging in your grandmother's grave for sadness, that only happens when your days are chock-full of happiness, when you are no longer scrambling. But, of course, I don't say this. I don't say anything.

"You know, Soraya, it was my countrymen—and women—who did away with that."

"Madam?"

"With slavery. If it wasn't for the abolitionist movement—my father was a member, a *force*, really—it would still be in effect."

"Yes, madam."

Something, no some*one*, whispers in my ear. *Amok! Amok!* And again: *Amok! Amok!*

It is plain that Mrs. Hattingh, taking out her embroidery, cannot hear them.

Amok, amok. The whisper becomes a chant, and then I see her, the Gray Woman, in the middle of the drawing room, wearing the uniform of a maid but with her face veiled. She pulls the scarf aside and grins at me, and I smile in return, knowing for certain now that she is Fatima.

Amok, amok, chants Fatima, saying again and again the word the slaves used as they ran from the farms to the edges of our city, through the center, setting fire to buildings, screaming for their freedom.

Mrs. Hattingh is smiling too. "A tireless campaigner."

Amok! says Fatima one last time, before commanding a piece of burning wood to pop so loudly in the fireplace that both Mrs. Hattingh and I jump. Fatima touches my shoulder as she leaves the room, while madam pushes at the fire with the brass tongs. Satisfied, Mrs. Hattingh turns back to me: "A great man, my father."

Her face is open, waiting, and I puzzle over what it is she wants me to say in response; it cannot be praise, for only children want praise for taking the right course. But still, the smile, the nod, the waiting, and I realize then that the true wonder of these people is this: they are perfectly at ease with doing the wrong thing for centuries and then expect congratulations for doing the right thing for a moment.

* * *

A small family for your people, she'd said.

Away from Mrs. Hattingh, elbow deep in warm foaming water, cloth against stone sink, slab of soap in hand, I think about the women on our street who have each carried a child every year of their marriages; some have up to ten, even fifteen babies. Not so Mama, for she is careful, skilled at knowing when her womb quickens, when it sleeps and even, though she is quiet about this, which tea to brew if a baby is unwanted. *A small family for your people.* The youngest, whom I did not tell her about, whose name I did not give, whose name I will never give her, the baby in our family, died of the foreigners' flu that came during the war years and took at least one child from every home in the city, rich or poor. When Baby was in her last week, my mother held her the whole time, didn't put her down once, covered her in prayers and poultices—cloths soaked in vinegar to draw out her burning fever—mixed her own milk with turmeric to give Baby's stomach ease, fed her tiny sips of rooibos tea on a spoon's edge to soothe her spirit, crushed chamomile flowers into her blanket to grant her sleep, spent her nights praying with us at home or with the whole congregation at the mosque, all the while bargaining, bargaining, *Almighty, if you let her live, if you let her live, I will fast every Thursday for the rest of my days. I will give up meat. Give up pleasure. Cook nightly for the poor even if I go hungry—hungrier—myself.*

It was for nothing. Baby was so thin by the end, a *slip* of soap. Still, when she died, it took three women, weeping, to prize her from Mama's arms, so that they could wash her body, rub it gently with oil and camphor, scatter rose petals on her kafan, swaddle her just as if she were sleeping. They told Mama she must accept,

accept, and when she cried out, *I won't! I won't!* the women were shocked; they reached to touch the wood on the table, the prayer on the doorframe, but then they agreed that it was not her—a pious woman—talking but the grief, which can drive you half mad. Later, I heard them say that it is always so when one loses a child; that there wasn't a woman in the Quarter, in the *city*, who did not know this grief or fear it, but that it would soon ease, it would have to, she had too much to do, too many to care for. But my mother's sadness sat deep in her, took her far away from us for a long time. She'd sit in the kitchen for hours at a stretch, a pot of food burning before her without her noticing, a rip in her skirt untended, my sisters' hair unbrushed, and she was staring, always staring, dazed, into the distance at something none of us could see. When eventually she did return to us, her hands were steady as ever at the pot, with the needle, the brush, but she was different too—she would move between holding us too tight, hugging us too close, and fading away, drifting elsewhere, a ghost in her own house.

At the end of next week, I think, tearing my thoughts away from Baby, another fortnight will have passed, and I will be able to go home again. What will I say this time to my mother about this job, about Mrs. Hattingh? Mama always poses a question with the answer she wants already built into it: *Everything is good? You listening to her? You remember what I told you?*

There's so little room to say anything, tell anything.

I look down and realize that my hands are raw from scrubbing. This petticoat must be clean by now.

I go outside to hang it up and walk straight into the glorious, heady scent of flowering geranium. I stand still, letting it flood my nostrils, seeing myself clothed in a red velvet gown, the waist pulled tight with a gold tassel, all gilt and crimson like Rosa. I must remember to take a cutting or two for Mama, for it is the geranium, she always tells me, not the rose, that is the closest we come to the scent of heaven. Where the geraniums are, so too are the saints. *Saints!* In Mrs. Hattingh's garden, no less.

Mama will put the plant's leaves and petals in a little jar filled with oil, stand the jar in the sun for one week until the oil is richly perfumed, strain it through a thin cotton cloth into a glass vial, and then, a single drop at a time, the oil will go into the boiling fat and ash from which she makes her soaps.

As always, when something reminds me of home, I have such a longing to return there.

Eight days is nothing, I tell myself, nothing at all.

Her excitement about her son's visit climbs as the weeks pass, so much so that she's practically dancing through her days. But when she receives another letter from him, this time with the "disappointing news" that his trip is two, perhaps even *three* months delayed, she takes immediately to bed.

"Soraya, I believe I'll rest today," she says, and that she wants only "thin soup and quiet."

When I take up the breakfast tray the next morning, I notice that the door to Birds is wide open, and when I go to shut it, I see why. Fatima is standing in front of the wall, hands on hips, looking at the scribbles in the animals' eyes, shaking her head and then picking up the hem of her skirt to try to clean it. A rage is coming off her, so strong I can feel it from the corridor, and I can guess why: Timothy or one of the previous owners' children must have done the scratching. Their youngsters are forever doing what they please, and it's the maid who pays the price. I'd hazard a guess that Fatima has a score to settle in every room of this house. Best to leave her to it, I think, and continue on to the master bedroom.

Mrs. Hattingh's face is drawn and ugly from bad sleep. She insists that I pull back the curtains, but when the light rushes in, she winces as though she's been splashed with icy water. She sets her eyes on the tray, not meeting mine, then works her way through the toast without taste or care, forgetting to put anything on it, voluntarily swallowing the bread cold, dry and crumbling. It's plain she does not want to leave her bed but forces herself to anyway—*if there is one thing I cannot abide, it's a layabout.* But when she gets up, the hours that follow are idle, listless, and she's absent in everything she does. *Heavy*, that's what she is, counting down the hours, full of bone-deep sighs and grateful relief when night comes and, with it, diluted laudanum to help her tumble back into sleep.

This mood, like a fever, lasts days, but when Mrs. Hattingh *does* rouse herself, she's like one reborn: cheeks flushed, movements strong—*A lesson from the war years, Soraya, the busier one is, the more swiftly time passes.* She goes first into the garden to prune any drooping plants. There's barely any green on them left by the time she's done. After that, it's back to work: she holds teas; attends luncheons; writes to papers, local and abroad, about war-widow pensions, library donations, and again and again to universities demanding that they open to women. She tells me that she's badgering the city officials about attending to the sanitation in the Quarter, that she wants to find out more about the local children placed in the camps.

It's better this way, I think; the more Mrs. Hattingh concerns herself with saving everyone else, the less likely she is to complain about the house or fret about how to make ends meet. (*I refuse,* she announces, when I find her balancing her books one afternoon, to ask my son for more money; London is so expensive, and now he's got the added costs of a long journey. Besides! I enjoy economizing—it's a challenge!) Yet when she is done with the world outside this house, she turns her attention back to me. Or, rather, to Nour. *Tell me everything about him, Soraya.* Has Nour sat his matriculation examinations? How did he fare in mathematics? Literature? Latin? Which of your two schools did he attend? . . . Oh, marvelous, I know the headmaster—a good egg, a credit to his race. Has he already applied to the Teachers Training College? She knows the chairman of the board, a Mr. Cartwright; if we ever need a word, they are on the Ratepayers Committee together.

As the questions roll one after another her mouth opens wider and wider. I stare as it grows, and her jaw becomes a large cave, her bottom teeth a circle of stools that surround her tongue, itself suddenly a red flame.

"Soraya? Know this. I stand ready to help Nour."

She could write to the chairman straightaway if I would give her the details! When I hesitate, she says crossly, "Never mind," then picks up Master Timothy's letter, complaining that I did a shabby job on the windows in the drawing room. I must not have used the vinegar mixture she provided; the panes are so foggy she can barely make out the sky. Again, please. Also, I've not yet made a start on the silver. Best begin! *Ticktock.*

The windows are *fine,* but I do them again. *See, madam, how obedient I am.* I go through every piece of old newspaper to wipe the panes dry so that when it comes time to restuff the gaps in the window frames, she'll have to ask me about it. And when that happens, I may or may not bring up my uncle, joiner to the governor, again.

Next, silver, every bit of it—what's left, anyway. *Look who's had to sell off all but two of the fish knives!* I draw my scarf across my mouth and nose to fight off the sickly smell of the polish. The remaining fish knives I leave out as though in error.

Anyway. Another fortnight almost done. I go home tomorrow.

FIVE

"I'm leaving now, madam. I'll be back in the morning."

"By eight o'clock, mind."

"Yes, madam."

"I'll see you out."

It's then that I see she's packed the knives away and stuffed one of the window gaps with her good writing paper. No doubt she'll dream up a punishment for when I get back.

I don't expect it by the time we get to the front door.

"Oh! I keep forgetting—mind like a sieve. Won't you open your bag, Soraya?"

"Madam?"

"I have to check it. I'm afraid we do not know each other well enough for me *not* to do it, my dear."

I'm surprised that beneath my fury I feel something else: hurt. She takes her time, riffling, peering, touching my things. As I watch her, an image of me bent over a tub of her delicates, my fingers rubbing her undergarments, the warm water sloshing through lace and cotton, rises before me.

"*There.* All done!"

I carry that search with me as I walk the city, as I cross from her world into mine. Carry it as I pass the old auction square with the block where people stood, mouths pulled opened, teeth tugged, arms checked for muscle. I carry it as I jump to avoid a carriage horse rearing up in fright outside the old slave lodge, as I make my way to the small squat houses that line Kings Street.

At the edge of the Quarter, where the cobblestones begin, I call out greetings to the women who stand on their stoeps, arms crossed, eyes on the street, and I tell the gaggle of children who tear past me to *watch it*, to *mind themselves*, I should go straight to my parents', but instead I dart toward Nour's family home, hot with hope that he too may be back for a Sunday visit.

"Haha! He's not home!" sings one of the young boys on the corner, and then he and his friends whoop and whistle that I will have to wait for my kisses. I spit at them and threaten them with a smack before going to the house anyway. Nour's youngest sister, a chatty girl if there ever was one, opens the door. Nour will be back next Sunday, she says, and the Sunday after that, and I should do everything I can to come home too. I tell her to tell him that next week is impossible, but after that—yes. *Yes.* It is only when I turn to leave that disappointment floods me: No Nour. No Nour. Not for another two weeks.

At home, Mama takes my wage envelope.

"Where's Papa?"

"At prayers at your uncle's house. He's been there all morning. Go and fetch him, he'll want to see you."

Back on the street, I hear the men praying just a few doors away, hear the murmur and song of their voices: devotion, declaration, witnessing, *Ya Rab!* My uncle's house is just like ours: thick white walls to ward off heat in summer and trap it come winter, wooden floors, a tiled stoep and a fig tree out front. At the door my aunt smiles, covers my face with kisses, invites me to sit with her, *sit, sit ma*, pushes a plate of sweet doughnuts toward me and says to wait for the men to be done, it won't be long, they're just in the back. She can tell, she says, lowering her voice, that it's not just prayers anymore; it's ratib.

I know then without looking what is happening:

A circle has been formed. The air is thick with incense smoke and prayer. The men chant, beat the drum. One of them gets up to stand still in the center of the circle. His body goes limp, the prayers thrum through and over him, his legs loosen, the sacred words run like water down his spine and he begins to shuffle, one, two, three, his torso in a shimmy, eyes glassing over, lips slack. Then he turns, as though bidden by something invisible, toward the two long swords in the room's corner, weapons from our life before. Fatally sharp, those swords, curved like a palm tree, weapons for a rich man, weapons for a holy man, weapons for piercing the veil between this world and the next.

He takes the swords, holds them aloft, then brings them down, cuts a shape into the air. I shrink into my chair as the chanting grows louder, for they must hold him up, keep him going. I can feel how he takes one of the blades and presses it to his skin, slices at his own chest, cuts deep into the flesh, and how they all, as one, wait for the miracle to come to pass. And it does, it does: There is no blood. None.

When they finish, it is my father who emerges first from the room. I go to greet him. He blinks when he sees me, as though still in the realm of the impossible, and tells me, beaming, that this is the fastest the Almighty has ever answered one of his prayers. We walk home hand in hand. I tell him that ratib always makes me worry so—what if someone were to hurt himself, what if the prayers don't work? My father smiles and says this worries him mightily too, and that each time his worry has been laid to rest. And more, each time he sees the miracle of bloodlessness, he's reminded that the body in the care of the Beloved is capable of transcendence.

At lunch I tell everyone about Rosa (but not that I can hear her).

"*Where* did you say the painting was? Which room?" Mama asks.

I'd already said where, but Mama, like me, loves to hear a worrying fact again and again.

"In her *bedroom*, Mama," I answer as my father shakes his head in disbelief.

"Where she *sleeps*?" Mama says. "No. No. I would not want that girl watching over me at night."

My father never draws people's faces, because it is forbidden in our faith, but my mother's discomfort is because she knows that even in death, people don't stop watching. And they don't forget.

"Imagine," she goes on, "letting that girl's thoughts spill out into the room while you sleep."

For the rest of the day, I do nothing. Mama makes my sisters run back and forth for me and allows me to speak, uninterrupted, for hours with my father. He shows me his latest rakams, his brow crinkling just a little when he tells me how much rice paper has gone up but how every day the need for our people's safety is rising too, so he works and works all the time. The beauty of my father's holy calligraphy has people clamoring for him to be the one to make the rakams they hang on their walls, the prayers they wear on their persons, talismans of protection, declarations of faith. But my father's rakams, I think dreamily, did not shield me from Mr. Edenburg, did not stop him from tugging at the chain around my neck, stroking the small gold box that holds the prayer, asking if all the girls of our faith were so modest.

It is night when my mother calls me into her room. She scoops a mound of hardened coconut oil from a little jar, and I settle on the floor between her legs. The oil melts, and her slippery hands glide through my hair, and that smell—musty, sweet, familiar—turns my body slack and my tongue loose.

"She searched my bag before I left the house today."

I expect Mama's anger, but all she does is shrug. "Never mind her foolishness . . . Thinks she's being clever, keeping you on your toes. The rudeness of some people. I wonder sometimes if they just don't know any better." She traces the pads of her fingers in small circles on my temples, and it is all I can do not to curl myself toward her, tell her I do not want to leave home in the morning, tell her there was more to my time at the Edenburgs' than she guessed and that, on occasion, Mrs. Hattingh and her old house frighten me.

Before bed, Lia, Alma and Kashif ply me with dozens of questions about Mrs. Hattingh, and in answer, I stoop, clutch my hand to my collar, mimic how madam plays with her long bead necklace, warble my voice, tell them how frightening it is to be in a large house surrounded by all this *wealth*, that life has been *so* difficult, that I have been *forced* to economize. Kashif, Alma and Lia laugh and laugh, and the more they laugh, the more I stoop, the shakier my voice becomes. By the time I finish, Mrs. Hattingh is twice her age and half as kind.

I say nothing to them about Gray Fatima or how Rosa can talk.

I have learned not to tell stories that frighten children.

SIX

"The season is turning!" announces Mrs. Hattingh happily as she walks into the house from the front garden, in one hand a loose bouquet of orange flowers, in the other a string-tied brown paper package. She lifts the flowers toward her nose, sniffs, then pulls a face: "I always forget these have no scent. They're so pretty, it feels as though God missed a trick. Do you know what today is, Soraya?"

"Yes, madam."

"Well, go on. You know what to say."

This has been happening for several weeks now. "It is just four—"

"No, *five*, possibly six months. Recall, please, that he wrote about the delay till December."

"Five, possibly six months till Master Timothy's visit."

He's excited too, she says, writing more frequently, telling her about everything he wants to do and see: ice cream on the promenade, cricket at his old school, mountain hikes and cold-water swims. In fact, the new arrival dates work out nicely! In time for Christmas, and the later he's here, the better the weather will be. Dead summer. He's also sent a little more money with this last letter, and with it she ordered a joint of fine beef that's just been delivered. She holds up the parcel, grinning.

Meat does not come often to this house—a mark of shame for her, but a relief for me—no steaks or joints or cuts stored in the icebox, no fussing over flesh and bone. She tells me to follow her to the kitchen, where I stand by as she puts the flowers in water and unties the string as though she's opening a gift: "We will eat like kings tonight, my girl." She looks admiringly at the moist red-pink flesh, the bright blood still oozing from the bone. She presses a finger to its flesh, delighting at how it hollows out, then springs back, evidence of its freshness. She beams.

My stomach turns. I don't mind eating meat, but the handling of it, raw, sickens me.

"*Look* at *that*. Almost worth its weight in gold." She's in a joking, jolly mood. "When I was a girl, I'd spend my summers on a farm in the middle of England, and they had a slaughter season for the lambs. Dreadful business. They *bay*, the lambs, before they're taken to the abattoir, as though they know what's going to happen to them. I'd hear them all the way up at the house, and sometimes my sister and I would run over and see them being herded onto the wagon, and each time my sister would have a go at freeing one. She was doolally about animals. I've never actually seen a slaughtering, though. Have you?"

"Yes, madam. At our house."

"At your *house*? Gracious, what a terrible mess that must be. And the *smell*. Your poor mother!"

I smile and say my mother doesn't mind. I don't bother to tell her that we slaughter only as sacrifice on a holy day of celebration, of penitence. The lamb is led up the cobbled lane next to our house—*come, come, come*—down the slim, shaded passage toward the garden, and there to meet it, standing beneath the loquat tree, a man with a knife, his mouth full of prayers and chants. You can never tell how the animal will behave; some trot forward in a daze, making their way to whoever calls them, eyes wide and blue. Others tremble, soft wool quivering. Then there are the ones that need dragging, ropes slung around their necks, tugged until the flesh beneath the hair is made red with roughed-up welts. The ones that resist are rounded up, captured. Boys, without instruction, mirror the men and circle close; the women raise their hands to their faces or lock eyes with the lamb, willing it to submit, sometimes shouting that fighting will only make it worse, that it is useless to quarrel with one's fate. But in the end, meek or a fighter, the animal will jerk its head, pull back against the rope, and the bleating turns to a baying that merges with the prayers.

Once, when I was very little, I lifted my eyes to meet the lamb's, watched them grow larger as the blacks moved from the center to the edge, and I heard it saying, clear as day—the words inside the bleats—*Spaaaare meeee. Spaaaaaare meeee.* I stuffed my fingers into my ears, shut my eyes tight, horror flowing through me, until I felt someone's hands tugging gently at my fingers, telling me to *look*, to look at her. It was Mama. She was crouching before me, and as my eyes met hers, I knew that she knew what I'd heard. *It's all right*, she whispered. *It's all right.*

I want to go, I told her, but she shook her head.

Soraya, you owe it your gaze.

"Soraya? Be sure to make a stock from those bones. If you start them now, I could have consommé for supper. Fatima always said it's bones that hold all the goodness."

I set to work. Wash my hands. Plunge the meat into a bowl, watch the blood marble the water. Rinse, pat dry. Place it on the chopping board. Reach for the sharpest knife. Offer up a silent thanks to the butcher for having already done most of the work, for I have no skill in carving, and each time I tell Mrs. Hattingh that I cannot do something she either seizes the moment to instruct me or despairs because she's reminded that I am all she can afford. I cut first into the soft give of the flesh, working my way alongside the bone, cubing the meat for tomorrow's stew. The bone with its marrow and still-seeping blood I place in a pot with salted water. Bay leaves, a quartered lemon and parsley dance on the boil. *Add vinegar,* Fatima advises from where she sits on a corner stool, legs wide beneath her skirt, *to draw out the flavor. And don't forget to invoke God's name. Make sure it's clean both ways.* Then, to my own surprise, I hold my hands over the pot and seal the broth with a prayer of thanks for Mrs. Hattingh, for myself, for the animal, while Fatima mouths the words along with me.

The broth is a success. As I clear away the supper dishes, Mrs. Hattingh sighs happily. "That was sublime. I could have had seconds of every course. I must write to my son immediately and tell him it was money well spent." She takes three quick sips of her wine, one after another. I look at the bottle; unusually for her, she's drunk almost half of it, and when she speaks, her voice is loud, bright. "Have you eaten yet, Soraya?"

"No, madam. I'll eat once I've done the washing up."

"Well, when you do, I wish you bon appétit. Do you know what 'bon appétit' means, Soraya?"

"That madam hopes I enjoy my food."

"That's the gist! Clever girl!"

I ask if I can clear her setting. She leans back in her chair, making room for me to do so, smiling, her eyes very small, and then says thoughtfully, "Tell me, Soraya, I know you can't read, but Nour, bound for teaching, can, yes? I imagine he's quite the avid reader and writer. At least, I hope he is!"

Three months I have been here, but I am still never sure what it is she wants me to say, what it is she wants to hear.

"Yes, madam."

"Just so. You know, I have been thinking so much about you two."

"Thank you, madam."

"It grieves me, Soraya, that you are so far apart." She knows, she says, that we are not always able to coordinate our days off and so haven't seen each other as often as we'd like. She thinks of us as the stuff, she continues, of romance and longing, a young couple sadly separated! "And there is only one way to lessen the suffering that brings. Do you know what it is, Soraya?"

I hesitate, then I say softly, hopefully, "That we see each other, madam?"

She gives a small laugh, shakes her head, takes another sip of wine. "That's a servant's response, Soraya. An answer for the body. No, my dear, I am thinking of something that soothes the *mind*, attends to the spirit."

She is playing with me. I see that now. As I place the dishes onto the tray, I grip the plates to get a hold of the anger I feel rising from stomach to throat.

"Can you guess what it is?"

"No, madam."

"Well, make *some* effort... Why would I have asked about Nour's reading?"

"I don't know, madam."

She puts the wineglass down with a sigh so deep it's almost a groan. "I thought you were a little more imaginative than this. All right. I see I shall have to speak plainly: letters."

"Letters, madam?"

"'More than kisses, letters mingle souls.'"

At the mention of kisses, the hot anger becomes a blush that reaches through my skull to the back of my head, setting my roots aflame.

"That's a quotation, my girl: the great poet John Donne, writing to his dear friend Sir Henry Wotton."

"Yes, madam."

"Good heavens, girl, there's no reason to be so overcome. Look up. Look at me! A well-written letter to one's beloved, be they friend, lover, child or parent, is among the highest expressions of love. My letters to and from my son have been, these last years, chief among my joys."

I'm holding the tray now, waiting for her to say something more, but she just stares at me, her eyes burning bright.

"Set the tray down. Good. I want to explain my thinking. You cannot read? That is correct?"

"Yes, madam."

"But Nour *can*. And well at that. And he can *write*."

I nod.

"Here is my offer: we will, once a week, meet in my drawing room, and together we will write your Nour a letter. You will speak, and I will take down what you say. It won't be exact—your speech is too simple to be interesting—but I will capture the essence of what you say. We can write about anything you like: your days here, what you've eaten, your parents' health, when you'll see each other. But there will be some rules. I will not tolerate any impropriety; nothing immoral will appear on those pages. You are an unwed girl in my home and care, and I take that charge and pastoral responsibility very seriously. We will not *send* a letter every week—perhaps every second or third—but we will sit together weekly to write one. I will not take the costs of the paper or the postage out of your wages. Yes, well, you may gasp. It will cost you nothing but will give you a great deal." She smiles. *"Well?"*

Her offer is unlike anything I could have imagined—her writing, her time, her promise to pay for materials and postage. My words in her beautiful script laid out for Nour to read. Generosity. Kindness! Even Fatima has a happy smile on her gauzy face. Then why this quickening within, a tightness in my stomach, a curdling in my throat? Am I that incapable of receiving goodness? The offer has been made, I tell myself sternly, as an act of charity. And charity is what she does. It is who she is. Yes, it may be the wine that has made her so full of giving feeling: I have seen over my years in these people's homes how their wine and spirits take them, turning love, anger, laughter, hotter, wilder. But all the more reason to say yes now before the glow of the drink leaves her.

Contact with Nour.

"Well?"

There is no reason to worry.

"I'm waiting. Goodness, my girl . . ."

Tell her yes. Do it now. *There is nothing to fear.*

"Yes, please. And thank you, madam."

I will say what I will say, and she will write what I will say.

"Wonderful."

The idea of the letters seems to excite her more than a dozen committees and almost as much as planning for Master Timothy's visit.

She chooses, as the hour for writing, Thursday at dusk—*The perfect time, Soraya, almost the end of the working week, ready for early posting on Friday.* I twitch a little at this, uncertain, worried, for it is an uncanny hour, the eve of the holiest day of the week, the hour in the Quarter when the faithful are called to prayer, when the jinn are abroad, when mothers call to children who are still playing to *come inside. Now.* The women hold open their front doors with one hand and wave their children in with the other. As the children pass, they each invoke God's name, because though jinn can travel easily between worlds, they struggle to make their way past a door locked by a key and held tight by prayer. For the child who refuses to leave his game, who waits for the sun to slip from sky to sea, there are warnings: *This is no hour to be caught outside, this hour when the jinn make mischief at best and dark trouble at worst. This is an hour when if you are not careful a man on a horse can appear and carry you off, far from your mother and father. Come in, come in now. If you stay outside, your face may freeze for the rest of your days, your mind may slow, your feet may hobble, for it is bad luck, bad luck to be out and about. Listen, listen to the prayers from the three mosques in the Quarter. How can you think to play with your friends at this holy hour when men of God do battle with the shaytaan for our safety?*

I do not say a word about my misgivings, because I feel, in the days before we first sit down, as though the offer were an egg on a spoon, and if I do or say anything it could fall, smash itself, be done for. Ever since Mrs. Hattingh suggested the letters, my missing Nour, my longing for him, has deepened. It's as though she's shown me a door, told me about the riches that lie beyond it, opened it very slightly, enough for the warm gold glow behind it to spill out, just a little, with both of us knowing she can shut it whenever she likes.

But she honors her promise, and that first writing hour begins as the others will: Mrs. Hattingh rings her small silver bell, calling out in a voice full of sweetness, *"Soraya! Soraya!"* My name echoes through the house until I appear before her, and she says, smiling, "Come, my dear. The hour is upon us."

She tells me to take the seat opposite her, and that is when I know for certain that the writing hour will be unlike any other at 23 Heron Place. There is the activity itself, but there is also this: we are, for once, at exactly eye level.

I do not exaggerate.

Consider how daily we sculpt ourselves: she sits for a meal while I stand to serve it; she inspects herself in the glass as I am on my knees dusting the skirting board; I am on a ladder washing the outside windows as she prunes her dahlias, her hands inside her gardening gloves as soft as the petals. Rarely do we see the world from the same viewpoint for longer than a minute, and yet for this hour we do, for this hour only our eyes meet evenly.

I say "I" and she writes *I*.

By my voice I am me; by her hand, she is too.

It is strange and wondrous, this alchemy by which we become not *one*, but each other: I speak my "I" into the room, the word takes shape in her ear, her head, and she commands her hand to scratch it onto the page: *I, I, I,* she, me, *I, I.*

When my father writes he rocks a little as though he is in prayer, which I suppose in a sense he is. When Nour writes, he hunches over the desk, head in one hand, the other grasping his pen, scowling, as though his whole body is working to make the letters. It has been so long since I wrote anything that I cannot say what shape I'd take, what marks I'd leave on the page.

Mrs. Hattingh sits straight as an arrow and writes quickly, easily. She does not stop; she rarely crosses anything out. She is fluently me from the first salutation.

It is that easy for her.

So, it is always at Thursday's dusk, when my labor for the day is mostly over and there is only supper left to serve. The bell rings, my name is made song—*Soraya, Soraya*—and she receives me with a smile.

I remind myself, always, as I take my seat, that there are things she does not know. She does not know about my own handful of years with the missionaries, with their iron rules and wooden rulers, their cursive, their kindness, their cruelty, their praise—*How bright you are, Soraya! How unexpected your capabilities. Our star pupil!* Their commands—*Stand and recite the poem for the headmistress, for the women who've brought their donations.* Their violence—*Bathe your hand, dry your tears. The wound will heal, but the instruction will last.*

Mrs. Hattingh also doesn't know that if I close my eyes, this could be any of the afternoons I spend with my father in his workroom, watching as he takes up his qalam, his knife close by to sharpen it, his pot of ink, shining black and ready. I'd steal in there, disobeying my mother's warning to leave him to his craft and calling, and watch as he worked, his focus absolute while he perfected the swoop and curve of God's name, or scripted a prayer so that together the words formed the shape of a flower, a tree, the cooling waters of a river. Sometimes he'd call me over, hand me the qalam: *Here, look, like this, try, loosen your grip a little, the words won't move through you, heart to head, if your fingers are so tight, that's better, good.* And though I never come close to his elegant skill—my text, through lack of time and practice, was ever clumsy, ugly even—I recall, constantly, his other lessons.

Beginnings, he'd say, these first moments before writing, *are sacred; a small glow in a dark room, the breath before the verse.*

"Are you ready, my dear? First, I must write the date, here in the right-hand corner, then the place. A new line for each bit of information: street, city, colony. You see? It is also a lesson for you."

"Dear Nour," I begin our first letter, adopting a formal tone I know she will want and he will chuckle at. "Greetings of Peace. When I am next home, I will go with my family to Bin Mikhail's shrine to pray for safe passage of those who are leaving for the pilgrimage."

"Of course. I've heard about your people's great pilgrimage, my dear—quite the journey!—but what is this shrine?"

"Oh. It's just a place we visit where an old priest is buried. We go on family days, an outing to pay respects."

She says how lovely it sounds, and I nod.

I do not tell her that the shrine is the grave of a great man, a man of unusual faith and uncommon bravery, a man who led a rebellion against slavery, who was captured by the settlers and sent to this colony as punishment, to a life in exile. I do not tell her that the shrine is the most beautiful place in this most beautiful city, that you must walk up ninety-nine whitewashed steps carved into the blue-gray mountain face, ninety-nine steps for the ninety-nine names of God, that the incline is steep but the air full of the bright freshness of gum trees, jasmine, eucalyptus and also the oil and smoke of incense. I do not tell her that from the top you can see through the trees to the drifting stretch of the turquoise ocean and that inside the green-and-white shrine the men are praying and the women are burning orange peel. I make no mention of the cats that weave and dart around the caretaker's vegetable patch, or of the women in bright festival scarves sewn with gold thread who watch their children laugh and play free. I do not tell her any of this, because she has no right to know, because these people who hold sway over our outsides have no right to know, to touch, our insides, and because this letter is for Nour, and he will know, he will know. I continue:

"After the shrine, we will go home, and I will tell everyone what I tell you now, that I am very happy in my new position with Mrs. Hattingh of Heron Place!"

"Oh, Soraya." She beams.

I arrange my face: stretch mouth, show teeth, crinkle eyes, beam back.

Lesson learned.

Easily done.

The writing of that first letter unlocks something in me. I cannot sleep and my body is ahum. Though the night air is cold, I fling open the window of my room. The scent of geranium, rich and potent, travels from the far reaches of the kitchen garden. I breathe it in, and a story comes to me. "Names and addresses have been changed to protect reputations," I say out loud, laughing to myself. I long to share it with Nour—with anyone! But there is no one to talk to, no one to tell it to. I look about for Fatima, but she is nowhere to be seen or felt. So the next day, when Mrs. Hattingh has left for a committee meeting to plan a picnic for unwed mothers, I go to Rosa.

"Once," I tell Rosa, standing before her without a broom or a cloth, not bothering to pretend I am there to clean. "Once," I continue, "there was a woman. She was called Soap Woman because she made soap. She lived in an ordinary house and lived an ordinary life. She was not special, but she would be made special, not by choice, but by fate."

At this, Rosa exhales, short and sharp, through her nose.

"She made soap the old way, from ash, and if you know ash" (*I know it,* Rosa replies) "you know there's no way to control it. The ash would cover her so she was always veiled, so there was always a layer between her and the world.

"'Making soap is a terrible business,' she told anyone who would listen. 'It is hot work and it stinks, and you must have the skin for ash and the stomach for slime.'

"But Soap Woman had a knack for it, for managing the long-roiling heat of the cauldron, the cooling and the molding. She had strong, deft hands, and at the end of the day, each cake of soap would be laid out in a row, perfect, precise.

"One day she was busy toiling in her yard when she had an idea: she would put three drops of precious geranium oil into the boiling fat so that it would smell, she knew, less of animal fat and closer to heaven and peace.

"She was right in the middle of soaking geranium leaves and scattering geranium petals (an old trick, she told a watching bird, that wards off the envious eye) when a woman appeared in the garden, wearing a thin blue robe that draped from her shoulders, around her head and over her arms. An outfit, Soap

Woman noticed, without beginning or end. Before Soap Woman could ask her who she was or what she wanted, her visitor began to sing, 'Geraniums smell of heaven and peace.' It was all so confusing to Soap Woman, because though she did not recognize the Visitor in Blue, and though this woman was speaking a language she did not know, Soap Woman could understand her perfectly. The Visitor in Blue went on, and everything that came from her mouth was a song: 'I know no peace and heaven / For I lost my family in a fire / I wear only blue to douse the flame / And I cannot tell you my name.'

"Soap Woman put a hand to her forehead, feeling a sudden wild heat, and realized that her neck and brow were drenched.

"'A fire! A fire! A fire!' the Visitor in Blue sang, and with each word, everything grew hotter, until it was so hot—the day itself, her body, even the ground she was standing upon—that Soap Woman could not even bear the word *fire* to be spoken, that she begged her to stop.

"'I will stop,' promised the Visitor in Blue, 'but first you must do as I ask.'

"'Anything!' cried Soap Woman, whose skin felt as though it were dripping from her bones and worse! Her soaps had begun to melt.

"'I want you to make the child I lost out of soap. You must carve her for me. She must have large eyes, a nose like a kitten's, soft hair, and wear a dress spun of finest cotton.'

"Soap Woman was shocked. 'I cannot make a likeness of a person, that is forbidden.'

"At this, the Visitor in Blue sat down with a sigh and said, 'I will not leave until you agree, and for every moment I am here and every time I say 'fire!' (and I will say it as often as I like), you will grow hotter and hotter, your soaps will melt and run down the gutter and you yourself will melt away, slink into the ground, turn to nothing.'

"Soap Woman knew her threat to be true, and so she promised, 'Come back a week from today and it will be done.'

"Satisfied, the Visitor in Blue rose and lifted her cloak, making it billow and curve, and as she did this, a cool breeze stole over the garden and the soaps' ruin was prevented. 'In a week,' she said, and smiled at Soap Woman before she walked away, the air cooling with her every step.

"Soap Woman worked each night: She boiled every scrap of fat she could find; she roamed up and down the street collecting ash from every neighbor who was home, and sometimes, if she was in a daring mood, even when they were not home. She'd walk right in and take the ash directly from their fireplace, without so much as a by-your-leave or a thank-you. At first, people thought there was some beautiful magic afoot: 'You come home and your fireplace is cleaned! There is a jinn,' they said. 'No, closer to a kindly ancestor, who comes and cleans your house when you are out.' 'No, no, not an ancestor, an ancestor wouldn't clean, it must be an angel,' they said. 'The Angel of Ash. A wonderful thing. A blessing,' they agreed. But in time, people saw that Soap Woman was the one stealing into their homes. First one person saw her, then another, and soon they told each other, 'This is no angel but Soap Woman.' Then the people realized that if Soap Woman was walking right into their homes, she may also see unmade beds and unwashed pots, and who knows what else she'd have a mind to take? And they spoke instead in outrage about the Thief of Ash.

"Soap Woman said nothing in reply, offered no defense" (*Good for her!* Rosa interrupts, and I agree, "Good for her!") "but Soap Woman noticed how easily an angel becomes a thief.

"And anyway, she now had as much ash as she needed. She got to work. She spent hours making molds out of various pots and dishes: this for the baby's middle, this for her limbs, this for her fingers curled softly against her mouth. It was only at the end of the promised week, when it was close to midnight, close to the hour of change and mischief, when the soap had cooled in the molds, that she risked scraping and carving the details.

"Making a baby from soap, she realized after a terrible hour, is impossible work. The limbs would not attach, the hands stayed formless, she couldn't give life to the face. Eventually, her arms aching, her fingers cut, her eyes straining, Soap Woman gave up and wrapped the parts of the soap baby in a blanket.

"The next day the Visitor in Blue arrived, bringing with her the heat and threat of fire. 'Where is my child?' She sang her question. Soap Woman handed her the swaddled soap-baby.

"The Visitor in Blue took it from her and held it to her breast. She cooed, then opened her mouth, and from it tumbled mother sounds: a gush of notes, a half-learned song.

"Soap Woman was suddenly worried: the Visitor in Blue did not seem to know this baby was not real. She was about to say this to her, gently, gently, when she heard something impossible.

"A small cry, rising up from the blanket.

"It must be the bird in the tree just there, or the Visitor in Blue has thrown her voice to make it seem so.

"Soap Woman leaned in and over to look at the bundle. There, perfectly formed, was the Visitor in Blue's child, back from the dead.

"'It cannot be,' she whispered.

"'Oh, but it is,' replied the Visitor in Blue as she leaned down to touch her nose to her baby, sniffing and saying, 'See, she even smells like geranium.'"

I raise my arms up, wide open toward Rosa. "You see?!" I say, my head tilted to the ceiling. "The miracle of love! The miracle of love! The miracle of 'I say so'!"

In reply, Rosa raises her hands. I have never seen them before; they usually sit on her lap out of the frame. She claps out her thanks for the story and when she is done, turns her palms up and cups them, as though ready to pray.

SEVEN

"'I hope that story brought you some amusement—worthy of a woman who bests an ink-stealing sailor.' Goodness! What a very odd thing to write. Whatever does he mean?" Mrs. Hattingh lowers Nour's letter to look at me, eyes twinkling and curious.

I have received two letters from Nour so far, and each time Mrs. Hattingh has taken his letter direct from the postman and kept it, sometimes for several days, until she is ready to read it out loud during the week's writing hour. And each time she stops to ask about something she does not understand, for Nour is writing to me as I speak sentences to him, in a careful code that holds our history. I look at her dull faced and reply, as I've done before, "It's just something we say in the Quarter," and this seems to satisfy her.

She does not allow me to hold or even to look at his letters for too long. "Enough now, my dear, you cannot read what he's written, so it remains just a square of paper to you. It doesn't do to make too much of an object for the object's sake—that's a slow slip toward idolatry. But I tell you what. I will keep the letters here, in my desk drawer, nicely together, safely bundled."

So I sit, dutifully, quietly, as she reads to me, hearing in her voice the trace and rhythm of my love's words. I have no way of knowing if she is reading me everything he writes. Instead, I must tolerate her being the bridge both Nour and I must cross, the troll we both must bribe.

"'Fondest wishes, Nour.' *Well*"—she puts down the letter—"I think he sounds most content on the farm, Soraya. What do you think?"

"Yes, madam."

"He'd say if things were difficult?"

"I think so, madam."

"Because I'd be happy to write to the farmer and intervene if anything untoward happens. It is important to hold people to account."

She scarcely notices that I don't reply; she's too busy packing Nour's letter away and readying everything—paper, pen, envelope—for my response.

Sheet angled, pen poised, she says, "Let's begin."

I say, as I always do, "Dear Nour, Greetings of Peace," and then I speak about my plans to crochet, under Mrs. Hattingh's instruction, a light cotton shawl for the summer months.

"It's a capital idea, Soraya. I'm so pleased you're willing to learn."

"Thank you, madam."

I go on about what I've cooked, the methods by which I've harvested, dried and bundled herbs, when I will next be home. Mrs.

Hattingh murmurs, nods, reminds me of this or that, as I talk and she writes.

"Shall I tell you something strange?" She stops taking down my sentence and fixes me with a long stare. "In the ancient world, it was the slave who could read and write, not the master. In those days, the educated were a little suspicious of texts. It was new to them, you see? To be well educated was to be trained in the art of memory, of recitation, of being able to hold the history of one's people and one's gods in the mind, not on the page. Even their muses, minor gods and goddesses of the arts, were in service to memory. Writing was a cheap trick. A convenience. You may wonder, Soraya, why I offer these little digressions: it is because I believe in education above all else, and I have begun to think of this hour as not only a means to ensure contact between you and your fiancé, but also as an opportunity for you to learn."

I want to tell her I know things about recitation, about holy remembering, about what cannot be touched by pen or paper, things that she may not know, but before I can, she gives one of her tinkling laughs and says, "Imagine, people thinking recitation is more important than a *book*."

Reading and remembering. Reading and remembering. Not two things, I think as her hand moves across the page, not for us, but one. From when I was seven years old, my father tutored me in just this, the memorization of the sacred through recitation. *Remember the prayer, remember the prayer.* If you commit it to memory, you become one of the prayer's guardians; it will not matter if a fire burns every page it is written on, if every house of the Beloved is pulled to the ground, if all our people are slaughtered but one, for the one who remains would have been taught to remember. The person is a pen. The person is the paper. The person is the holy book's memory.

"What is this word?" my father had asked me that first day, pointing at his script.

"*Proclaim*," I replied.

"Not only *proclaim*. Also *read*, *recite*. You see? For us, to read, to recite, is one. For a long time here, before I was born, our people were not allowed to write, so we wrote in secret. And the recitation became even more important."

"What would happen if someone was caught writing?" I asked him.

"Oh," he said, a small pause as he pinched the brush between his fingers to drain a tiny drop of ink back into the pot. "A punishment. Of whatever sort they felt like that day. Sometimes very bad. Sometimes not."

"What else? What else could we not do?"

"Whistle."

"*Whistle?*"

"Sing," he went on. "The women were forbidden to wear patterned kerchiefs, only plain ones. Speak our language. That's why none of us speak it today." And with a laugh, he gestured at his own sandals. "Wear closed shoes." Then, "Be outside after sunset."

When the slaves were freed, my father told me, the sunset curfew was lifted. "That's why your grandfather was so fond of walking late and deep into the night. He would wander for hours as if every step in the dark meant more than what it was."

"And what about the Lodge, Papa?" I asked him, knowing how he crossed the street to avoid that building and how, if ever he did happen to pass it, he kept his eyes down, drew his children close, offered up a stream of prayers. My father was silent, so I pressed: "Did your father live there?"

Eventually, he said, "Not him. But those before him. And no one lived there." He paused. "They stayed there." And then, dreamily, his eyes unfocused, he said what I could not understand: "There was a dark corridor that led to a courtyard, and in the courtyard, a well where daily they drew their water and sometimes tried to jump into, as though the well were a tunnel that could take them home. And each night, the women would be made to line up and wait for the sailors to arrive, rough at the door, coins in hand."

I was seven. I did not understand. I do not know what else he would have told me if my mother had not appeared in the doorway, her body outlined by the rush of bright light behind her. It was only when she said, "*Khalil, Khalil,* what are you telling the child?" that my father twitched as though being roused from sleep, looked up and seemed to recognize just whom he was speaking to. "Outside, Soraya," my mother said, "and shut the door behind you."

I did as I was told. Almost.

I lingered at the door, scrunched on my knees, my eye pressed to the keyhole. My mother was bending over my father, stroking his head as though he were a child himself, saying, "No *sense*, no *kindness*, in telling her those things."

My father nodded, then brought an unusually shaking hand up to my mother's face, blinking, blinking. He stroked her cheek, promising, "No more stories of the life before."

But that, I think now, doesn't mean that the stories didn't arrive unbidden. They had a way, those stories, of curling in your mouth, stopping your tongue, holing up, then spewing out. Like this: One day my father emerged from his workroom, as always, adrift between two worlds, taken by one of his strange fits, where he sees either too much or too little. We were sitting around the kitchen table, my mother, my sisters and me. In the center, a large bowl of salt to make spiced pickles. I was taking the salt up by the handful when, without warning or explanation, my father smacked it hard from my hand, sent it scattering white across the floor. It was years later I found out that once, when his grandmother had been whipped, the farmer had taken salt and pressed it into the soft, burning give of each of her open, running wounds. A punishment, people said, that was worse than fire. When he was done, the man said she was fortunate, because although the salt was meant to hurt, it was also the thing that would clean her wounds.

"Soraya?"

"Madam?" I come back to this room with a start.

"Answer me, girl. I've asked you twice now: Would you like me to teach you how to write your name?"

"Yes, madam. I'd like that very much."

I will, I realize, have to disguise what skill I have and let her teach me as though from the very beginning.

"We'll do that next week then."

She pushes herself back from the desk and walks over to the drinks cabinet, where she pours herself a thimbleful of brandy and drinks it in small, wincing sips. She places a light hand on the tabletop and turns her head so that I can see, even in profile, a tight smile forming.

"Tell me, Soraya, and be honest: Have you let him kiss you yet?"

My mouth dries; my stomach and cheeks heat up. The question is a crimson bird, flying through the room, cawing. I shake my head before words are able to form.

"We won't mention it in the letter, of course, but you can tell me. Have you let him kiss you?"

"No, madam."

She gives a little laugh. "Why not? Is he ugly?"

"No, madam."

"Well then?"

"It—it wouldn't be right, madam."

"Wouldn't it?"

She's playing with me.

"What would be right then, Soraya?"

"To wait, madam."

"'To wait, madam.' What good answers you give."

"Thank you, madam."

"But a good answer is not always the right answer. All the poets write about wanting to kiss their beloveds. Wouldn't you like to tell your beloved how much you want to kiss him? Telling is not the same as doing. 'How I long to kiss you,' you could say, or 'One day my lips will touch yours.' It wouldn't be improper, I promise. You have my permission. I could help you find the words."

"No, madam. Thank you."

"I can't imagine anything he'd like to hear more. There is a world of difference, my dear, between the chaste declaration of affection in a letter and the disregard of virtue in the flesh. I promise"—and here she appears to be stifling a laugh—"I promise I will hold the line for you. Nothing infra dig."

She turns back to the drinks cabinet and, with a lightly trembling hand, tries replacing the glass stopper to the bottle. "*There*," she says triumphantly when she manages. "Well? Shall we?"

"I—"

"Oh, never mind." She makes a fuss about lighting one of her rare cigarettes, tapping it, bringing a match to it, inhaling, eventually saying, "I forget how sheltered your sort are. Off to bed with you. I'll address the letter later. I'm tired. It wears one out so, this constant holding of others' feelings and dreams."

I bid her good night, offer my thanks and tell her I will see her in the morning.

Alone in my room, my back against the door, I conjure up the last time Nour kissed me, a farewell kiss, before I came to Heron Place and he went back to the farm.

"There," he'd said as I laughed against his lips. "Let that take you through your week as surely as it will take me through mine."

Then another kiss, this one stronger, a clamp, the shock of his tongue tracing the edge of my mouth, then pressing, pressing for my lips to open, one hand on my neck, a finger digging into the nape, the small hollow between my hair and scarf, my body growing hot and slack, and running all through me a longing to grab back, hold tighter, open wide, take him by the arm, the mouth, the head, for us to flee up the hill, past the cannon, down to the water.

She may write the letters, place her voice on top of mine, but she does not know what it is to hold or be held by him, does not know him by smell or sight or gait: the small mole beneath his right eye, the pale scar on his left hand, the black curls that grant him—already tall—inches more in height, his stumbling clumsiness, unchanged since he was a skinny boy.

"Unbearable, unbearable," he'd whispered in my ear. "Another month before I see you. Maybe more if they say I need to stay. But once we're married, all this will change."

No matter the busyness of the week, we meet for the writing hour.

There are times when I cannot think of what to say, but Mrs. Hattingh is quick to tell me that a short letter is better than no letter, that there have been times when this dull little city has provided her with almost nothing to share with her son, but that that was half the battle, half the *fun*, finding a way to make the uninteresting interesting. At the end of each hour, once I've signed off, she packs the pages away to address and seal in her own time. "And now, a letter to Master Timothy," she'll say as I'm leaving the room. She's not mentioned the kissing again, and I notice that she's lately stopped drinking wine with her meals. She's also returned to this back-and-forth: *Do you know what today is, Soraya?*

Yes, madam, it's just three, possibly four months till Master Timothy's visit.

She is girlish on posting days, dressing for the walk as though it were a Sunday, putting on her fancy hat with the silk cabbage roses, eyes keen and bright, tut-tutting about the cost of the stamp but always saying, *Never mind the pennies; a promise is a promise.*

At the next letter hour, she announces that from here on out, we will begin not with writing, but with reading. She has a whole heap of books, she tells me, and gestures to the pile she's made on her desk. Sonnets, novels, plays and prayers: it will take us *years* to get through her selection, she says, and smiles. She picks up a book, opens it to the marked page and then reads in a ringing voice a poem about a woman in a tower weaving a web, who sees a passing knight, falls in love with him without ever speaking to him and eventually ends up dead and floating down a river. Mrs. Hattingh is so moved by her own performance that when she finishes her voice is throbbing, her eyes are glistening and her nose needs dabbing.

It's dark by the time we get to the writing, but she is energized, eager, saying the poem has "inspired" her. I am surprised at how her hand flies across the page even when I am not speaking. When I ask about it, she reminds me she is "rephrasing," just as she had promised she would, taking my speech from the "banal" to—and here she searches for another word, finally offering "lyrical." "Shall I read it back to you?" she says.

I nod.

"You said, 'The loquat tree in my mother's garden is full this year.' The best that can be said of this is that it is a sentence that holds a piece of information. But it is not the stuff of letters, certainly not to one's affianced. I have taken the baldness of your language and burnished it thus: 'The loquat tree that grants my mother afternoon shade has once again had a bountiful harvest—its luscious golden fruit lies scattered around. Mrs. Hattingh tells me that this fruit first arrived on our shores as a seed in a Chinaman's pocket, and though few eat it by itself—it does not rank high here in the Cape, where we have such an abundance of excellent fruit to choose from—it can be pickled as a local treat.' Do you see what I did there, my dear? I stayed faithful to the essence of what you said but weaved all sorts of things into it. Like conversation, letter writing is an *art*, one that should hold facts, digressions, ideas and affection, but still be a true reflection of the person writing it. That last bit about the pickling comes from something you told me a few weeks ago. Be warned!" A small chuckle. "I am always listening."

My breath draws sharp. I have once or twice suspected before that she is leaving out this, making more of that, but *this*? I don't know where to begin: My mother doesn't have time for "afternoon shade"; the fruit is collected before it falls and we eat it regardless of where it "ranks." What else has she changed? What else does

Nour receive and puzzle over? I stretch my mind now, trying to remember what he has said. What she has *said* he has said. But she keeps his letters to me, so I have no way of checking.

Mouth dry, I say, "Please, Mrs. Hattingh, can you just write what I say?"

"Well, this is certainly not the response I was expecting. I am only trying to help you."

"Yes, madam, but—"

"I wonder if you understand the *effort* it takes to transform what you say into something readable. No, no, that is a foolish expectation . . . Why would you? How could you grasp the labor involved, the psyche summoned? It involves a traveling of intellect and spirit, an abdication of the self, almost as though I am dreaming while awake. I have to let the words run through me. I make myself a channel, a bridge between two worlds. I see your eyes have grown large at the thought, as they should! I've been doing it as a kindness to you and I haven't told you the full extent of it to spare you any further feelings of indebtedness to me, but I see now that I have, as ever, been generous to a fault. From now on, I will write things down exactly as you say. A secretary, no less. It is up to you to refuse the ancient gods of art and writing. I am just a vessel." And with that she takes up her pen, dips it into the inkwell and crosses out everything she has written, line after line. "*There.* Is that better?"

I'm looking down at my hands. I have angered her, that much is clear, and I need to make things nice again. I admit to myself now that I have come to rely on those letters and that I thought I'd bested Mrs. Hattingh in the deal—that I was giving away nothing but telling Nour everything. That when I said, *The loquat tree in my mother's garden is full this year*, he knew I was saying, *Remember how* we ripped the stiff, dark leaves from the branches and sailed them down the gutters in winter? That when I said, *Perhaps she will make blatjang soon*, I was also saying, *Remember how we stole a jar, ran up the hill, ate it all while we watched the harbor full of ships take boys to war? Kiss me. There is no one to say you can't.*

I'd thought myself so clever, daily thinking up things to tell him, imagining ways to tell her as little as possible.

"*Well?*"

"Madam?"

"Shall we make another start?" She takes out a clean sheet of paper, places it in front of her and repeats, "'Dear Nour, Greetings of Peace. The loquat tree in my mother's garden is full this year.' That is sixteen words. I will write them exactly so and you can count them up if that makes you feel better. Perhaps I can help you even make out a word or two for confirmation."

She writes the sentence and then turns the page toward me, a finger hovering over each drying word. "One, two, three..."

"Thank you, madam. That's all right."

She raises a hand to her head with a wince. "Let us finish this next week. I feel one of my headaches coming on. They arrive only during times of great strain."

Disappointment travels through me. "Can I bring you something, madam?"

"Just some tea, Soraya. I have not mentioned it, I have not wanted to worry you, but I have not been sleeping well. My doctor tells me again and again that I need to rest, not overdo things, but I maintain that a life of service to others is a life well spent."

"Yes, madam."

I leave to fetch her tea and think how just this morning I'd noticed her bedroom candle burned down to the wick—she must have forgotten to blow it out before she slept. She could have burned the house down while I slept, thinking I was safe in my bed in the garden room. Imagine! This house all aflame, fire bursting from her bedroom window, shattering the glass, her bedding and nightdress catching alight, her whole body a burning log.

PART II

EIGHT

The District. Its market. First light. The hushed stillness of early morning stretches over the long main street with its tall, askew buildings that hold small flats and hundreds of souls, new shops and old prayers, and soon, a jostle of people from every corner of the earth, curious songs and curious folk, trade, trade, trade, fruit and fish, copper and women, fabric and cures, salt for meat, salt for curses, salt for cures, a jangle of notes from an upright piano, a snatch of a song, a horse grunting *no, no, no*, a rhyme to sell oranges, the oblong notes of a prayer chanted from a minaret, carpenters, church bells, washerwomen, factory girls, errand boys, and, between them, teachers and the doctor, our doctor—loved, beloved, a fez on his head—and those two lawyers who make trouble for the governor, they chatter-chatter, call-call, shout-shout. Mostly poor, though not all poor, some walk rich, their boots good enough to *clickety-clack* on the narrow pavement even as they weave between streetlamps and street merchants.

I am here, basket in hand, list in pocket (for alone I am a reader again), because Mrs. Hattingh has sent me to buy her fruit and spices, old Fatima's supplies having finally run out. I'd told her both could be found in abundance and at a good price in the District, and she leaped at the chance to buy cheaply and well. So here I am, on Jubilee Street, just as day has begun. It is a relief to be away, even for a few hours, from Heron Place. I take from my apron pocket Mrs. Hattingh's list; as always, she'd insisted I memorize everything on it to prevent errors or theft (by myself or the shopkeepers, she does not specify). I still haven't told her that I can read, and so I have to mind when she hands me these bits of paper that I don't glance at them in a knowing way. She has been "teaching" me how to write, first their alphabet, then my name—*Everything starts with one's name, Soraya.* While my script was not very good to begin with, I have played the novice and pretended to know next to nothing. The last letter, she'd slid the closing page over to me and told me to sign my name. *That's certainly an improvement!*

I'd cocked my head modestly in response.

The District is not very far from my own home, and I have been often enough to visit—to buy this or that, to see festival parades on the Big Days—and each time I've marveled at how very different it is from the Quarter. *Our* streets are bound together by faith and family, whereas the District is a place, not of one way, but many. A shabby place, to be sure, and just as my home is, it is mostly for us poor, for lives packed together, a place of tight corners, small squabbles, sharp struggles, of arguments on stoeps and no way to ever be alone. There are the same frantic feuds and unexpected kindnesses, the same easy stabbings and scared children, rats scurrying about with disease, and yet still a scrap of something being found for the cat that's caught no mice that day. There is nothing about it that is clean or lovely, nothing of the quiet beauty of Heron Place, *a slum*, the wealthy among the settlers call it, but there is *talk* here and faces that move through these streets bearing no resemblance to one another except that they are all people. It's on these streets that you'll see a Jew next to a Chinaman next to an African and, close by, an Indian and even, if you look carefully, you'll see the natives of this land, still holding on—nails torn and bloody from holding on. These folks jostling against one another make do, find a way, keep at it, sometimes all those things in a single moment. And if you look at the children, you'll see how they've been made through love or force or seawater voyages. Why, I have even heard tell of a Japanese and an Egyptian opening shops right next door to each other! In the Egyptian's, they say, there are tiny glass bottles painted with swirling pale-gold flowers holding precious quantities of fragrant oils—neroli, jasmine, rose—as well as packets of dusty hard-gum frankincense, small discs of coal that gleam hot orange when lit, copper water pipes with snakelike tubes from which to puff and forget and while away the hours. Next to that shop, they say, is the Japanese place, where nothing is sold, but things are *taught*. There are classes where men learn how to fight as gracefully as they might dance and break wooden blocks with their bare hands. But I have yet to see either, and these may just be tales the Quarter people make up about those in the District.

 Mrs. Hattingh had asked last night to come with me—*It is so many years since I went to the District, Soraya,* she said, her voice full of longing—but I'd gotten up early on purpose and made only a very small effort to rouse her. She'll be very angry about this, but I want to be alone here, not walk a step behind her.

I'm so sorry, madam, I could not rouse you, I will tell her, and then cast my gaze to the vial of brownish-red laudanum next to her bed, and she'll be too ashamed to say anything.

The street has begun to trade. If I am lucky enough, I will find a little spot where I hear only unfamiliar tongues—just nonsense, no-sense words to me—and then I will feel myself drift through and out. I will be gratefully somewhere else. For the sameness of Heron Place is suffocating, and lately not even my stories can rescue me from it. Even with the weekly letters, the hours between there and home stretch out, and I am lonely with just an old woman and house spirits for company.

I cast my eyes about and see across the street a woman tied to the pole, her eyes blank, dress falling around her thin-thin shoulders, her movements jerky, tugging at the rope like a dog. I remember her from the last time I was here, when I'd raced over and tried to free her and was told, *Stop, stop right there*, by everyone all around. She's a *loco*, *malkop*, they said to me. She's poor old Christine, raving mad, and if not tied up she'd be running into danger, doing God knows what with God knows whom, that she was put there by her family, so that she could at least see and talk to passersby while everyone else in her household was off working. Better than being confined to a room, tied to a bed, available to every criminal, everyone told me. She was mad, yes, but like this, she was still in the world, safe even. Don't worry, they had said, someone always makes sure she has water, a piece of fruit or bread. Malkop Christine bends down suddenly from the waist, half her body hanging off the other half, arms outstretched, gray hair matted, long, falling in front of her face, all the while yammering away to something about something. People stream past her, moving to the side, leaning back, lurching forward; one man gives her arm a gentle pat, and she bellows out, still bending, "Good morning!" but another mischievously pinches her on the behind, and at that she veers up straight, first bares her teeth, then screeches at him like a banshee. The man leaps back in fright and holds his hands up, ducking, half mocking in his apology, and it's only then that I see what her hair and body have been hiding and what no one else seems to see or notice: a small goblin, ugly as sin, a quick way about it, on spindly legs marked with tufts of fur, ready to follow his malkop mistress's instructions. She mutters to it while keeping the bottom-pincher in view and then sends the goblin after him, bounding down the street. This man, I know, will have no understanding, none whatsoever, about why his day's luck is about to turn so mercilessly bad. I let out a laugh and look around me, still surprised that no one else can see it racing down the street, and then I realize that Christine is staring at me. We lock eyes, she knows that I know, she sees that I see, and she grins, then does a little dance. This one, I realize, didn't bother waiting for death to become a Gray Woman.

Behind me a door creaks open, and I turn to see in its frame our doctor, taking his leave of a patient. Doctor stops to offer some comfort; a man is holding a small child to his chest, who is taking short, shallow breaths, listless, bright cheeked, dull eyed. A woman—it must be the mother—stands beside them, weeping into the edge of her long scarf even as Doctor says nothing is certain, *not yet, not yet*, and perhaps God and medicine can work together. He presses a bag of lemons onto them, urging them to eat one a day, and then gives them also what I think are handkerchiefs but then realize, as the mother holds one to her face, are masks. How strange, I think, as I watch her tie it, see half her face disappear behind it: for two years we wore masks just like that one every day, and now we walk as though our uncovered faces have always been safe for us, safe for others. I remember Baby and the foreigners' flu that took her and offer up a prayer of my own for this little one.

A man wheels his fruit and vegetable barrow out in front of me and shouts that I should mind his path! I shout back that he has no business on the sidewalk, but when he pushes on, it's my luck, because one of his mandarins falls to the ground and rolls right up to my skirt. Ha! I take it for myself, its wobbly orange skin cool against my palm, and I find a corner to peel and eat it in.

In this moment I am perfectly happy. So much so that I laugh and wave when a gang of boys charges past me, making their way onto the back of an ice cart, one pressing his tongue and dirty face against the big block of ice, another hacking at it with a pick, all ignoring the man at the front who swears at them in a stream of Cape tongue. Ahead of me, a woman who fancies herself a politician stands on an upturned fruit crate, a gaggle of people around; she speaks about not trusting the settlers and taking matters into our own hands. The men watching her surprise me because they look without sneering, they listen without jeering, and when she raises her fist and shakes it above her head they join her, crying, "Aye! Aye!" A few doors down two men carry an upright piano between them, shuffling their feet as they manage its weight, edging sideways into the spanking new turreted cinema, where already—so early!—folks are lining up to get their tickets for the afternoon show. And there is the building of Nour's college-to-be, where he'll talk late and long into the night with the other students, all of them thinking-fighting-dreaming for our people.

The fruit's citrus smell sinks rich and deep into my fingers, and I place the peel into my pocket. I will dry it out for a day or two on the kitchen windowsill, and when it has the feel of stiff bark, I will grate it into a powder and put it in the glaze for cardamom doughnuts for myself and Mrs. Hattingh. She'll like that.

But now, to the spice shop, left at the corner, a few paces down.

A tiny brass bell announces my arrival, and inside incense burns steady and smoking. They know me here, for I have come often before with my mother, and one of my father's rakams hangs on the wall. I look at it now, his calligraphy positioned carefully to face those who enter the shop, to ward off any malice or bad-think, to stop unkindness or jealousy in its tracks. The Indian has placed his daughter at the counter, and she looks up with kohl-rimmed eyes to greet each customer. Her head is covered with a wisp of fabric, a soft shimmer of cream chiffon, the hair beneath it shining with coconut oil. One piercing in her nose, two in each ear, and, on her right wrist, three thin gold bangles. Behind her, row after row of thick glass jars of spices keeping cool, dry and dark in this cave of a shop. The Indian's daughter has a brass scale before her, weighing each purchase with a sure, deft hand and the precise eye of someone used to ciphering. I wonder what it is to be her, to sit here each day, far from the sun. It is luxury, I think, to own your own shop, to be your own master.

The daughter offers me our greeting in our holy language, for we are of the same faith, and I return it, wishing the same peace on her. She recognizes me and starts to measure from memory what she knows to be my mother's usual order, but I stop her to say I have come for my new mistress, an Englishwoman, and she promptly puts down the jar of dried chilies and, with a knowing smile, reaches for the white pepper.

"No," I say, "she wants curry powders."

"They all do these days. Does she want one that's already mixed?"

"What do you have?"

The daughter laughs and offers up a jar. "Give her this one if you don't like her. It's called 'Mother-in-Law's Revenge.'"

I smile and say that my employer is a kind woman, and besides, she's told me what she wants. The daughter says that is good fortune indeed while I take out the list and begin reading, making a show of it—she may be sitting in her own shop, but I can do this! As the girl picks out the first jars—scrolled cinnamon, bay leaves, ground turmeric, whole coriander, black peppercorns, cumin—and begins to weigh, she asks, "What is your madam's name?"

"Mrs. Hattingh."

"Which Mrs. Hattingh? Salt's Edge or here in town?"

"Town. Heron Place."

"*That* one." Her mouth goes tight and she shakes her head and makes herself very busy with measuring everything out.

Who is *she* to say anything about where I work or whom I work for? I must pull her up short.

"Why you being so rude?"

"I wasn't!"

"Must I take my business elsewhere?"

"To *where*?"

She's right to ask: there isn't anywhere else close by, and she knows I know that, but I can't let other people speak about Mrs. Hattingh like this, so I push. "I'll tell your father how rude you're being about customers."

She looks worried and insists that she wasn't, I insist that she *was*, and round and round we go, and she says she was only thinking of me, that if we don't look out for each other, then who will? And I think this is a bit much because it's not as though we *family*, but something about how she looks tells me I should hear more, so I say she better tell me straightaway why she made that face, and she backs off and says, "It's nothing, nothing," but I say I'm not going *anywhere* till she tells me, and she throws her hands up and says that a girl who lives on her street went to work at Heron Place and she left after just a few weeks because Mrs. Hattingh was a strange one—up and down, up and down—that there's something wrong in that house, everyone knows it, and everyone in the District has heard how even the old lady's own *son* would rather stay in faraway London Town than come and see his own mother, even after he'd lived through their world's worst war, and what does that mean except that there's something very wrong in that house? And she's not saying it will be the same for me, but her friend didn't last out the month.

I want to laugh. "Is *that* all?" I say. "Tell me something I don't know."

Now she's riled up too, not a girl who can stand being dismissed. "I also heard that he's maybe a bit touched or he lost half his face or something."

"What?"

"Her son. Her London son. And his mother can't stand to look at him the way he is now so he stays away."

"You want to watch yourself. That's Master Timothy you're talking about. *Lieutenant Hattingh*, in fact. And how he is and where he went are no concerns of yours!"

She shrugs in response. "If he's even still with us."

"That's a *wicked* thing to say!" I picture the soft-eyed boy in the photograph. "To even *think*. What is *wrong* with you?"

I'm startled by how furious the gossip about Mrs. Hattingh and her son makes me, but I can't work out if I'm angry for my employer's sake or because I worry that some of it, any of it, might be true.

She's starting up again about how she wishes no ill on anyone when the door swings open, bell tinkling, and another customer walks in. She and the Indian's daughter greet each other warmly, which confuses me, for she is a European woman, but then I remind myself: this is so often what the District is like. I look curiously at the woman and note that though she and Mrs. Hattingh share a skin tone, they are nothing alike in sound or dress. This woman's voice has a rich song to it, now rising, now falling, and she is wearing a large scarf wrapped around her person, covering her head. From behind, I might have taken her for my mother. She asks us, chatty and chummy, why we both look so cross, and I'm stunned when the Indian girl starts to tell her about Mrs. Hattingh and Heron Place as though she—a stranger! not one of us!—has every right to know. I tell the spice man's daughter to be quiet and that she shouldn't share my business, especially with one of them, and the European woman laughs at this and says that she is Irish: "I know things about the English you couldn't dream of."

I assure her that I could. I say this so forcefully, so crossly, that she cocks her head, takes a step back. "I don't doubt it, my dear . . . If I were you, I'd throw some salt and hang dried sage at every door in that house."

The Indian girl raises a hand to the ceiling, testifying, agreeing, *Salt!* So now it's the two of them, united, in telling me about my affairs. I have been burning miang stokkies in my room once a week since I began at Heron Place. I know exactly how sad houses summon the dead, how often a roaming spirit is blown in through my door, delivered at my feet along with dried-up fig leaves.

"Salt," the woman repeats before turning to pick up a bag of rice, and I pretend to not hear her.

I look at the turncoat Indian girl and I do what my mother

would: I make my expression pious-like and say that I am not one for idle gossip and certainly not malicious rumormongering. The girl insists that she is not either—"God forbid! *Kassam*"—she is just concerned for this family, just as the Almighty instructs her to be. I raise one brow just a little and, summoning my softest voice, tell her that every family has its trials and it's not for us to judge, and turn to leave. She calls after me that she's just trying to help, and I turn to say that I pray God forgives her for telling tales. The Irishwoman says that she hopes we'll see each other before long. I do not reply.

My anger carries me at a brisk pace back to Heron Place, and all the way I'm wondering why on earth I defended Mrs. Hattingh, why I didn't ask more questions, why I feel sorry that her son's living far, far away has become, in the eyes of the city, her fault. And what if there is some truth to it? A boy who won't come home. A boy with half a face, a face his mother cannot bear to look upon and that he cannot stand to show her.

I get back to find her waiting at the front door ready with a scolding, and my feelings of fond protectiveness vanish. "We *agreed* that I would accompany you to the District!" she cries.

I answer just as I planned that I could not rouse her, but without the laudanum to glance at, this does nothing to stop her upset.

"I consider this most unkind of you, Soraya. You know very well how much I was looking forward to going."

Why, I think, does she need to go there? It's not *her* place.

Her voice is quivering now, her handkerchief at her mouth. "When I think of all I do for you, the effort I make to bring you some joy, give you some comfort—" She bites off the last words and then waits, as though expecting me to list her many kindnesses.

"I'm so sorry, madam. We'll go together next time. I was very wrong, very wrong indeed, not to wake you."

"*Well?*"

"Madam?"

She ushers me inside with a look of hope and longing and says, "Tell me what it's like now."

"It's—"

But she cuts me off before I can say any more, her words tumbling, a frenzy: "The District has always struck me, Soraya, as the only bit of this little city that is uniquely itself. Everywhere else looks and feels like a smaller, more primitive, sunnier version of home. But the District . . . why it's as though I'm wandering the markets of Marrakesh, seeking out the souks of Cairo."

It cannot be reasonable to feel this amount of fury toward her. She is only trying to be *nice*. She has traveled. Seen things. Say something kind. Tell her how right you're sure she is—Marrakesh! Cairo! Say the names of the places you dream of and will never go. Come now.

But I can't. I don't.

Instead, I stand very still and say without much feeling that the District is no place for a lady, that it smells quite terrible, that the drains are in disrepair, that each overcrowded house contains a person sick and that since the war the children are filthier than ever and swarm about like an ever-moving stench. I show her the spices, saying I've brought the best-smelling thing about the District back with me and that if she needs me, I'll be in the kitchen preparing supper.

She is stunned by my response; I so rarely offer anything but bland obedience. I expect some punishment, but instead she just stands there, holding an opened jar to her nose, sniffing, and the more she sniffs and sniffs, the more I can hear the Indian girl saying, *Something very wrong in that house.* Mrs. Hattingh finally stops and looks up at me with an ear-to-ear smile.

"It's amazing, isn't it, Soraya? I smell this and feel as though I am suddenly elsewhere. Perhaps this is the truth of those Eastern tales about the genie in the bottle, perhaps this is the magic."

I don't answer, because what is there to say? I understand in this moment that every woman, rich or poor, madam or maid, dreams of escape.

NINE

I've been bothered morning, noon and night by what the shopgirl said. Not because I believe any of it (I've seen the letters Timothy writes his mother, and more, I know how people here talk: they make up seven stories out of two facts and swear up and down that each one is the truth), but I've grown frightened of his room all the same. An afternoon with his things now means a sleep of nightmares, and I race through my tasks, finishing so quickly that Mrs. Hattingh says that she finds it difficult to imagine the room has been cleaned correctly and for spite bids me do it again. *And Birds. And* Fontana. Today, as I beat the faint traces of a week's dust from Timothy's school blazer, I resist the urge to pray, cover my head, remove my shoes, burn orange peel. I ask only that my heart stills in my chest, that my hands stop their trembling, that my breathing steadies. I will myself to work slowly, carefully, to look at everything. *There is nothing to fear. Nothing to fear.* I turn out the collar of his school shirt and see that his name label is still there, sewn in, I imagine, by Fatima. I flick the toy soldiers over one by one, then set them straight again. I look at his collection cabinet: there are small rocks by the dozen, a dried-out wishbone, coins, a photograph of him with friends. *Look at them, I tell myself.* Five boys in all: the three kneeling are laughing and holding cricket bats, Timothy scowls into the sun, his arm around the fifth boy. At the back of the photograph, their names: *James Bradford, Antony Ramsay, Harold Cunningham, William Lockday, Timothy Hattingh.* Next to all but Timothy's, in a hand I recognize as Mrs. Hattingh's, a different date and place: *12 December 1916, Verdun. 3 September 1916, The Somme. 2 November 1916, The Somme. 17 July 1918, The Marne.*

He has so many books, Timothy. A shelf full. Usually, I just wipe them down, but today I choose one, trace a finger lightly over the raised gold lettering of its title, turn the first page, then the next, reading with a smoothness I didn't dare hope, sentence after sentence. A girl, her brothers, their dog, an attic room, a boy who never grows up, a mother who keeps a kiss hidden on the side of her mouth, a father who worries about how to provide for his children, a ship that sails through the sky.

At some moment—or on some page—I ceased standing and am now sitting, feet on Timothy's bed, the duster in my hand grown limp, forgotten. Sink, sink, for this is a slip into a stream, pebbles underfoot, a cold rush of water, of words, a walk in a forest, suddenly a clearing, a new place, a waking dream. No instructions here, no *wash this, take that, mend, scrub, fasten, cook, tell me, give me*, none of that.

It is only when I hear her calling, "*Soraya, Soraya,*" that I yank myself back, jump onto my feet, pack away the escape from the pirates and call back, "Yes, madam!"

* * *

Dear Nour,

Happy birthday.

Mrs. Hattingh's pen skids across the page and she looks up, mouth wide, eyes glittering. September 9 is, she tells me, also Timothy's birthday. He is twenty-two today. His letter a few weeks ago told her about how he planned to celebrate—first, a light supper at a fancy restaurant, then a show with his sweetheart. Has she told me about this girl? No? Oh, well, there's not much to say just yet, he's said very little himself and she's simply delighted he's found someone. Doesn't it sound like a splendid evening—the supper, the show? An evening of hats and dancing and taxis. How she *longs* to be with him. There is no decent theater in this sad little city. She sighs and looks out onto her garden, then asks, "How old is Nour?"

I do not answer immediately, because the shock that they were born on precisely the same day in the same city—the one still here, the other so far away; the one into nothing, the other into luck that not even a war could undo—is mine too. I fib and say that his birthday is actually a few days away, that Nour is twenty-one, just two years older than I am. I do not know why I lie, only that I do not want Mrs. Hattingh to feel any further kinship with him. It is enough that we share this hour with her.

She stares again at nothing in particular. "Nour did not enlist?" I hear the judgment in her voice before she softens, saying, "Oh, but he would have been just a year shy. Timothy volunteered as soon as he turned eighteen."

I want to say, *No, of course Nour did not enlist to join your stupid war. And if he had, he would not have been given a gun to defend himself.*

For all her reading, this small fact has escaped her, this demand that our men be both as fearless as gods and as expendable as pack animals. It occurs to me now that Mrs. Hattingh must ask and ask to know about my life, but I know the smallest details about hers, from her menses, scattered unevenly throughout the year, to the plates she loves best, to how hot she likes her bath.

I watch now as her hand works across the pages. She is smiling as she writes, pausing to admire her own penmanship, taking care to blot any drops of ink. Ever since I caught her changing what I say she makes a big fuss of reading the letter back to me: *There. You see? Exactly as you asked. Poetry be damned!*

On letter days we are both lighter, happier, and it begins to bother me that our moods are so approximate. In the last month her concern for what happens outside the house has grown dimmer, and she has ceased most of her other correspondence.

Our letters, it seems, are enough.

She's having lunch at Mrs. Cunningham's, she told me this morning—*Though her cook is not a patch on you, Soraya!*—and after lunch, they'll go for a walk. *A constitutional.*

She's probably on the promenade still, parasol in one hand, bag in the other, hat tilted just so, her friend by her side. For once she's not set me additional work, and I wander the house, hearing my own steps, seeking a task, a distraction. I could go into Timothy's room to read, but I've a restlessness in me that wants something else, someone else.

In Mrs. Hattingh's room, the afternoon sun casts a window of light and shadow on the floor. A breeze moves the net curtain, and Rosa raises her eyebrows at me by way of greeting. I walk to the dressing table, peer into the mirror and then trace a finger over what's there: the glass-topped panel, the mother-of-pearl-backed brushes and powder puff, the jewelry box with her "good pieces." I take her brush to my head, then tug out any of my telltale hair. She's left out her laudanum bottle again, and I play with it, pressing the stopper, sucking up what's left, holding tight while I release it back into the vial, drop by blood-brown drop, measuring how many nights' worth she has left.

Rosa slides her eyes over to the adjoining dressing room and then, with a small smile, cocks her head.

I spend hours in here every week, hanging up Mrs. Hattingh's pressed and ironed dresses, folding her undergarments, dusting shelves that hold shoes, handbags and hats. There's a pigskin box labeled COSTUMES that I've avoided touching until now. I cover my fingertips with the edge of my dress and fling the box open. It's full of frippery: scraps of satin, silk flowers, strings of colored beads, scarves beaded and tasseled, gold bangles and rings, headdresses studded with stars and glass rubies, harem pants. When Mrs. Hattingh used to go to pretend parties, she'd go as one of us—or, at least, her idea of us.

I take a silk flower and fix it behind my ear. Place rings on my fingers and a good number of bangles on my arms. I stand before the long mirror in her bedroom, turning my head this way and that, raising my arms, dancing a slow, wavy step.

Rosa is watching, smiling, nodding.

We look more alike than ever; anyone, even we two, would be hard-pressed to tell the difference between us.

I lift my skirt and prance about the room, one of our people's songs on my lips, about a ship arriving on our shores and the young women who must weave their reedbeds to prepare for the settler sailors. The song is usually sung at a fast clip, the pace to disguise what awaits the girls; the men who sing it usually rush through the verse like maniacs, their heads bopping up and down, shouting that the ship is *there, look, look, there, it's coming!* but I've always thought the song should be sung slowly, that the sighting of the ship should go out like a sigh across the sea, that the weaving of the mats is no less than a funeral chant, a keening, the wind at our door with bad tidings. It is a story of what is coming, that there is no good lying just ahead, no good from when the settlers dock and knock. Never any good comes from that.

None, agrees Rosa, and then, briskly, *Pack away, quick! Madam will be home soon.*

"Mrs. Cunningham has asked a most unusual favor of me. I should have refused—and no one would have judged me if I did—but I felt bound by years of friendship and my own good fortune . . . Never take a long walk with a grieving woman, Soraya, there's no knowing where you'll end up."

I take her coat as she unwinds her scarf along with the rest of the story.

"You remember my friend Mrs. Lockday, who lost all four of her boys at the Front? Here, gloves. *God*, this wretched pin . . . The one who had the woman come to her house and perform all sorts of nonsense—tapping on tables and burning incense to summon the boys' spirits? Yes? Well, Mrs. Cunningham has gotten it into her head that she wants to do the same for *her* boy, and she's asked *me* to play host because her husband forbids it. I said to her, 'Hang on, how can you be sure he'll turn up at mine? Wouldn't he find it easier to make his way home?'—really, the leaps one has to sometimes take! But apparently, the fact that he used to come here so often to play with Timothy will be enough. School chums. Harold stayed in the trenches while Timothy became a pilot. What else could I say but yes? It will be a tea next week Tuesday. There'll be five of us altogether: Mrs. Cunningham, Mrs. Ramsay—the one who did those terrible talks that upset everyone—and Mrs. Lockday. She's *insisting* on coming too . . . says the seer is *her* find. And she's bringing her mousy sister." Coat, hat, parasol, all put away, she turns to worrying about the menu. "What am I going to put out? Tea. Watercress and egg sandwiches. And apple charlotte! Cheaply done and difficult to get wrong . . . Also Master Timothy's favorite, so good practice for you because I'm sure he'll want it when he's here. But for God's sake don't mention *that* on Tuesday. Those poor women, those poor mothers."

When I open the door to Mrs. Cunningham, it's all I can do not to burst out laughing, for the seer with her is none other than the Irishwoman from the spice shop, the interfering know-it-all who'd issued me instructions of salt and caution. She's a step behind Mrs. Cunningham, a large carpetbag over one arm and a fold-up table under the other. Our eyes meet; she gives a small smile and a little shake of the head, and at once I know that she's asking me to not say a word about our having met before. Mrs. Hattingh comes striding down the corridor, hands thrust out to meet her friend. She kisses Mrs. Cunningham and, upon seeing the size of the seer's bag and furniture, teases, "Goodness, have you come to stay? Come in. Come in. We're in the drawing room. The others are already here. Soraya, will you take . . ."

"Miss Turtle, ma'am. Miss Kathleen Turtle."

"Will you take *Miss Turtle* to the kitchen for a cup of tea before we start?"

They may depend on her to contact their dead, but it's tea in the kitchen for her.

"Yes, madam."

Miss Turtle drinks two cups of tea (three spoons of sugar a cup) and tucks into several slices of bread spread thick with the butter I've only just churned. I manage to move my mother's kumquat jam from the table before she catches sight of it, and make a show of wiping up her crumbs. When she realizes there'll be no more food forthcoming, she says, "Well, I best make a start," and digs into her bag; out comes a wreath of starched cotton flowers, strings of beads, a belt strung with silver bells—perhaps she too had an employer with a costume box. All is piled onto her person: in moments she's draped in flowers, beads and bells that tinkle as she walks.

"That noise will likely scare off the dead," I say as I lead her to the drawing room, and she laughs, good-natured.

"Not to worry. They'll come through. They always do."

"I'm sure it helps that you have some foreknowledge of everyone here's sorrow."

It's a spiteful comment to be sure, but she's unmoved, serene even, and replies with what I've thought often enough. "It's a wonder, isn't it? How much we know about them and how little they know about us."

"First, the candles," Miss Turtle announces, handing a taper to each of the women, saying they must work together to "illuminate all." The six of them move solemnly around the room, setting each wick alight. The curtains are shut tight against the late-afternoon sun, and Mrs. Hattingh makes another joke, this time about how all this candlelight will make them look ten years younger. The others say nothing; they are quiet and sad. Miss Turtle sets up her table; on it a bowl of salt, a vial of holy water from her church, a small wooden crucifix and a pile of little stones she says she's brought all the way from the "old country." Mrs. Hattingh's guests eye the table warily; they are all good Christian women, and they know that even with the cross of their faith on that table, they are dabbling in something they shouldn't.

There are seven of us if you count me. A good number, my mother would have remarked, for a gathering of this nature. The women arrange themselves around the room, with Mrs. Cunningham taking the chair closest to Miss Turtle's table, then Mrs. Lockday and her sister beside her. Mrs. Ramsay, who has kept her hat and gloves on, sits pinched on the edge of the room's most upright chair, her gaze fixed on something none of us can see, and my employer busies herself with plumping cushions, handing out tea, asking if anyone would like clotted cream with her cake.

"It is time," says Miss Turtle.

The women turn to her as one, and Mrs. Hattingh, smiling, sits herself down.

"I will not cast the stones just yet. First let us see who comes through and what they have to say."

Miss Turtle holds her candle up above her head, invoking her saints, asking Mary, full of grace, to come to us, stay with us. She walks the room three times, asking for blessings and protection to fall as soft as rain upon those gathered, for the spirits that rise up to be the ones we seek and for those who have not been called to stay at rest. Then she goes from chair to chair, sofa to lamp, *sniffing*, a dog after a bone. Sometimes she stops, eyes shut, body swaying, nose toward the ceiling. The women watch her, hands at their mouths, eyes glittering, bodies tense with longing while she says regretfully, "No. No, nothing here. Not a breath. Not a whisper." This goes on and on, her sniffing and stopping and swaying and telling them there's no sign of anything, the women holding themselves first tight with hope, then stooped with disappointment, until she reaches a worn-out armchair—the only one with no one sitting in it—right by the fireplace and says, voice low and urgent, "Spirit tells me I must stop here. Spirit tells me this was the boy's favorite chair whenever he visited."

A gasp ripples through the room, and Mrs. Cunningham, a believer before she even met the woman, cries out, "Yes! Yes! That was where he loved to sit. Isn't that so, Alice?" To which Mrs. Hattingh smiles: "Quite right. In fact, the boys would always make a dash for that chair—see who could get to it first."

Well, who wouldn't have? I'd hazard a guess there are fewer more comfortable places to recline in the entire city. I have eased myself into that seat a dozen times when Mrs. Hattingh was out. Miss Turtle knows people, that much is certain. She looks up and around, and her gaze settles on mine. I have been so taken with watching her that I'd forgotten to still my face. She stiffens, rolls her eyes a little before fixing them into the distance.

"Spirit has come," she says, very softly, "and Spirit says there is a *skeptical* presence that will make it difficult for the boys to come through. Spirit asks that the unhelpful person leave the room of her own will."

Then she goes to the center of the room and turns slowly, arms outstretched, eyes closed, as though in a child's game of blindman's bluff, to root out the culprit. Sure enough, she stops at me. I put a hand to my mouth to prevent a laugh flying from it. She points a finger, one eye cracked, and says, her voice rising, "Spirit says it is *this* person. Spirit asks this person to leave."

I don't need to be asked twice and make for the door. I've no need to watch the rest of this sham unfold, the trance to come, the consolations: *He is resting! He feels no pain now, he felt no pain then!*

But Mrs. Hattingh stops me. "I'm sure you are mistaken. Soraya's people are very spiritual indeed."

I know then that Mrs. Hattingh wants me to watch, to witness, so that she can talk and talk and *talk* about it with me after. Miss Turtle shuts her eyes, pinches the bridge of her nose with two fingers and jerks her neck as though she's being moved about by some force within, before saying, "Spirit says she can stay." She eases herself into the empty chair, eyes still closed, clutching the chair's arms, murmuring, "Are you there? Travel now toward us, gently, gently, for your mother waits to greet you. Your mother waits to greet you."

At that, a low moan enters the room and we all stiffen, as though of one body. We turn to one another and realize that it is no ghost; it is Mrs. Ramsay. Her eyes are glassy with tears, and she has that same stare as always—as though she has arrived from a thousand miles away. She rocks to and fro, the moaning growing louder, with the sound seeming to come up from her stomach—or from the center of the earth. Her hands are pressed together, and it is Mrs. Cunningham who says what we are all thinking: "Good *God*! Are the dead speaking through her?"

Miss Turtle goes toward her, crouches down, places a hand like a nurse on Mrs. Ramsay's forehead, stares deep into the other woman's eyes, strokes her tight hands and says, "Nothing of the sort. You're just so very sad, aren't you, my dear?"

At this, Mrs. Ramsay's moan becomes a rough sob that builds to a howl. Her cry fills the room and climbs to the ceiling. Mrs. Lockday and her sister move toward each other, and I can see that Mrs. Cunningham is starting to panic, likely fearful that all this will scare off *her* boy. She raises her voice over the crying: "My dear, please *calm* yourself. If we are temperate in our manner, perhaps the boys—" But when she says "the boys" she too begins to weep: *Harold. Antony. Boys. A ball. Scabbed knees. Down in the garden, ever so long ago . . .*

Miss Turtle, watching all, says in a deep voice, "Lighten your hearts and dry your eyes, for your tears made a stream for the boys to sail on . . . While you wept, a young man entered the room. I do not know whose son he is, but I will describe him and you will be able to claim him if he is yours.

"He is so very tall," and she tilts her head back as though gazing at an invisible giant. Mrs. Cunningham and Mrs. Ramsay both shake their heads no, their boys were not so tall. In response, Miss Turtle lowers her neck, indicating a medium build, and says, "Ah, that's better, he's coming into view now."

The two mothers, dark heads streaked with gray, lean forward again; perhaps, perhaps, they will meet their children.

Miss Turtle looks at their heads and says, "He has dark hair, like a blackbird."

The women sigh—neither's boy was dark haired.

"No, I misspoke. I mean like a sparrow, a brown sparrow, and eyes with a twinkle."

The women lift their eyes, hopeful.

"What a handsome fella he was!"

"What color are his eyes?" Mrs. Hattingh's voice rings out, and I can't help it, I grin. She is always a woman after a fact.

"I cannot say. I'm seeing as though from a distance. Perhaps they are green . . . No. They are brown. With a touch of green. Or green with a touch of brown. Flecked, they are."

Mrs. Ramsay, I think, is going to faint, for the flecks are the thing that make him one dead boy and not another.

"It's *Antony*," Mrs. Ramsay says, so fierce and certain that Mrs. Cunningham murmurs, "I suppose it is only right that he would visit here too. He and Timothy were such chums."

Miss Turtle claps her hands together with delight—*Antony it must be!*—and tells his mother that he is in a field of daisies, running, running, with a lovely dog—did he have a dog? Yes! Yes! She turns to promise Mrs. Cunningham that *her* son may yet make an appearance, that she'll ask Harold to come through right away. This time she sprinkles salt all around and asks the women to form a circle, to join hands and to pray, just as she does, that Harold is able to travel over and through from the Great Beyond to greet his mother. Pray! *Pray!* They do as they are told, with Harold's mother swaying, begging, calling his name again and again, and the others joining her until his very name sounds like a keening.

Who in this world—or the next—would answer to this mad call? I think, and I'm right, because for all their chanting exactly nothing happens. Eventually there's only silence and slumped shoulders, and Miss Turtle says to accept that Harold does not want to make contact today. The women turn to comfort Mrs. Cunningham: Mrs. Lockday with assurances that her moment *will come*, Mrs. Ramsay— giddy, transformed—to say that when it does, she will *know*, and then insists she, not Mrs. Cunningham, cover the seer's fee. Mrs. Cunningham, too disappointed to answer, does not argue.

I put out the candles and open the curtains to the early-evening light—let me do what I can to hurry this charlatan along.

Mrs. Hattingh and her guests are talking to and over one another, and that's when I see Miss Turtle stop in packing away her things, stiffen and put a hand to her lower back as though a pain has just struck her, murmuring, "No rest. No rest." She shakes her head as though to clear what she is seeing, but her words continue, along with a little laugh: "No rest for the wicked, Mama, no rest for the wicked."

"What was that?" says Mrs. Hattingh, sharp-like.

Miss Turtle's eyes are shut and she seems to be struggling to open them. Her neck is twitching, left, left, left, and she puts a hand on either cheek to still herself, repeating, "Hail, Mary, full of grace. Holy Mother of God, I call upon you. I call upon you."

"Who is it? Who is it now?" whispers Mrs. Cunningham, but Miss Turtle just snaps open her eyes, smile wide.

"All clear! Just some strays, my dears. Nothing to do with anyone here. Now, who is it that be settling my fee?" To Mrs. Cunningham, still aquiver with hope, she says, "Now that I think on it, it was likely your boy, come to tell you that he's well and resting. At peace. 'I'm at peace, Mother,' he said!" She breaks off and looks around the room, her voice a little shaky. "But I can't do any more today. I'm tired . . . It would help if you each made an altar for your boy. Put a candle beneath his photograph and say a prayer daily. Those who have been through war, it is harder for them to find quiet . . . the guns still ring in their ears . . ."

Mrs. Hattingh, who has been staring at her tight and hawkish, cuts in: "What a clever idea! Thank you so much for your tremendous efforts. Soraya, please show Miss Turtle out."

As I close the door behind me, I hear my employer say in her smiling voice, "Utterly *fascinating*. But does *every* Catholic remedy require an altar?"

* * *

"I used to do what you do."

She's stripped off the jangling bells, the crown of flowers, the beads.

I put another pan in to soak. Should have done this first thing this morning, but it slipped my mind because of the afternoon's tomfoolery. From the corner of my eye I see Fatima moving around the pantry, keeping herself busy-busy so she doesn't have to deal with our guest.

"You won't get that grease out with just hot water," says the seer. "Do you have bicarbonate of soda?" She points, unseeing, to where Fatima stands. "There should be vinegar in there too. We'll lift that in a jiffy!"

"I know."

"Ah! The secrets of the trade. I used to be you, but Spirit had other uses for me."

From the pantry comes a soft laugh.

"I'm sure . . . Did you lie about hearing their sons?"

She fixes me with one of the stares she used for the ladies. I thought it was a trick earlier, but her eyes are as dark as stones, impossible to look away from. My father has this power also, though he does not use it like this. "No. You hear him too. Feel him about even though he's far off. Restless, even in his sleep. Still half here, though he lives there now. But my business is to comfort. That's what I'm tasked with."

She lifts her eyes to the little window at the top of the doorframe.

"I told you at the shop you should hang something there. Perhaps on every door in this house. See if she'll let you . . . You take care, my dear. For all her laughing about this and that, she's troubled day in and out, and when you live with someone like that, your own wits become tangled too."

TEN

My next Sunday home, Nour is not there again, and I find myself unable to tell my mother about the letters or the séance. Instead, I complain that Mrs. Hattingh's house is a strange place full of fright. "Sometimes I think I don't want to be there anymore. I want to find something else."

"What you mean," Mama snaps, "is that you cannot bear to *work*. There is nothing wrong with Mrs. Hattingh; your work is easy, *light*. Think on what it could be—a house full of children, men, demands. You are lazy."

I turn a sulky face away from her. I am *not* lazy. If I were to work with my *father*, I told her, I would rise hours before the dawn, I would work joyfully late into the night, I would fast every Thursday, *I would, I would* . . .

My mother looks up, bewildered. "Are you still so very young? You can't do that. Come now, do not act the child."

"But I'm not happy there!"

"*Happy?*"

"There's something wrong with the house . . . and with her—"

"You listen here, Soraya. You have a fanciful mind. That's fine when you're a child and when you want to daydream life away. But you're not leaving that job. The Edenburgs were a different kettle of fish. This time, the wage is fair and that woman has done nothing wrong but miss her son."

"Mama—"

"No!"

"Well, maybe she'll find reason to let me go."

Mama grabs my wrist, holding me tight enough to hurt me, and says to *look at her*. "Don't you do a *thing* to make her upset! You hear me?"

"I *hear* you. Next door can hear you! And you're *hurting* me."

"All right! But you can't leave there. I can't wash like I used to. I'm tired. Your father's slowing down also. You don't see how tired he is? You want to get married, you want a wedding, you want to not work, you want everything. I'm going to have to send your sister out to work. And Kashif too."

"Lia is too young!" I say, full of fright for her.

"Same age as you were when you went. We need the wage. You understand me?"

"Her son will be visiting soon."

Mama pauses. "There will be a man at the house?" she says, tilting her face toward the ceiling.

"Yes," I reply, also looking up and not at her.

"There's a bolt on the door to your room?"

"I told you there was," I answer, remembering nightly dragging the small chest of drawers against my bedroom door at the Edenburgs' to stop the master from coming in, while the scullery maid who slept in there too pulled her sheet up to her chin, shaking.

Mama shuts her eyes. I can hear and feel her working to steady her breathing.

"Mind you use the bolt. Mind yourself."

"Yes. Fine."

"Soraya—"

"Yes. *Yes*. I'll mind myself."

"Come. I need to prepare supper."

In the kitchen I watch as she measures the rice and dried beans with the precision of someone counting mouthfuls. She's even taken down two of the three jars every bride in the Quarter receives on her wedding day—one with rice, another with sugar, the last with salt—and looks set to dip into them. I ask what she's doing, for the jars are not supposed to be opened—they are for blessings, for luck: rice for full stomachs, sugar for life's sweetness, salt for protection—but she doesn't bother answering me. Her jaw's tight, eyes tired, and I notice for the first time how very gray the hair at her temples has turned, how worn her scarf looks, how even in anger her movements are slow.

That night, in the deep quiet of my parents' sleeping house, I wake up. A dream had roused me—I was in a forest, but one beneath water, a forest on the ocean's floor where lemon trees swayed next to giant kelp and rosebushes were surrounded by starfish. The seawoman of my childhood stories walked beside me, and as she turned, her robe transformed into a fish tail. She swam ahead, calling to me over her shoulder. I could hear her words traveling to me as the water moved and stirred. She said, *There is a room you have not yet seen.*

I wake up trying to answer her, but hear instead the rise and fall of voices. I climb out of the bed, my sisters still sleeping, and creep down the corridor. It's my parents, awake despite the hour. Their bedroom door is open, and I stand in my white nightdress, scrubbed so clean by my mother that its edges shimmer brightly in the moonlight.

"... I tried talking to her, but there's never any way of knowing which way she's going to go. She doesn't stop to *think*," my mother is saying.

"Well, she's young."

"No such thing as young when you're in a stranger's house. No such thing as young. And it's not just that."

"What is it then? What troubles you?" My father's voice is soft, worried for us all.

"She believes her own stories so. She's always been like that. And now she's got something into that head of hers about her madam. Soraya's nonsense, up to her old tricks again."

"Then maybe we should bring her home."

"Fine words. Home to no food?"

"We have food."

"For now."

"Rest. Rest. More work will come to the house. It will come."

"She is right that Lia is too young to work. And Kashif too."

To this, my father is silent. And then there is another sound, one I have heard so seldom I almost didn't recognize it, of my mother crying.

"Come, my dear, it will be all right. Let me kiss your poor hands. I know how they ache."

I can't hear her anymore; she must be weeping on his shoulder or else she's put a hand to her mouth. It is unbearable then and now, this secret softness between my parents. I slip back to my bedroom, vowing as I hold tightly on to Lia that I will put aside any unease, any anger, about Mrs. Hattingh, stop my stories even as they form, hold down the job, bring food to our table, be uncomplaining, unsuspicious, good. *Good.*

ELEVEN

Ever since the séance, Mrs. Hattingh's made a habit of stopping by the kitchen at least once a day, always making out as though she's there to discuss the supper menu, but really, it's to talk about her son. You'd think she'd have run out of stories, but it seems she can go on and on forever; sometimes she'll repeat a story but with one new detail that she makes much of, or she's found something in the story to feel more deeply about. She's stopped talking about his life in London (except that she's "concerned" that his young lady may delay his visit further) and now tells me about his boyhood—bicycles, boarding school, scrapes, high jinks, standing bravely by his father's graveside. As she speaks, I ask myself, just as the shopgirl did, what manner of family this is. Yes, they write to each other—Mrs. Hattingh tells me morning, noon and night about his letters—and yes, he sends her money dutifully each month, but it's been *four years* since he was home. If there is something wrong with his arm or his eyes, his mother could find someone to help him while he's here; if the right side of his face is gone, she could look at the left. Only once she mentioned that he'd been in the hospital for a long stretch—not an ordinary hospital, but one for the boys who were very "nervous" after the war. But she didn't dwell too much on this and I didn't press her, because what do I know of such places?

The lingering's started. I expect to hear another story about him, but instead, she has questions about me, one after another: How am I liking working here, and how is my mother's health, and is my sister going into service too, because she has a friend who is looking for a likely girl and she'll gladly help to set up an interview, and am I still enjoying having a room all to myself?

I respond quickly: "Happy, thank you, madam . . . In good health, thanks be . . . Not yet . . . Yes, madam."

I think that's the end of it, but she pulls out a chair, sits herself down at the just-scrubbed table and makes a big show of closing her eyes and inhaling with a big smile on her face.

"Goodness, that smells heavenly! What are you making?"

"Tomato stew, madam. With the lamb offcuts, just like you asked."

"Oh yes, of course. Another one of your mother's splendid recipes?"

"Yes, madam."

"What a gifted cook she must be."

"Yes, madam."

"I love the *economy* of Cape recipes. Nothing is left to waste."

"No, madam."

"Humble ingredients, ingenious methods. A kind of magic, really." Then, in a teasing voice, "Are you a sorceress, Soraya?"

I smile. She wants something. That's what's going on here. And she wants me to open the door a little, even if it's just a crack, and ask her what that something is. Well, I won't.

"And once it's at the boil, do you keep it there?"

"No, madam. Now I must bring it down to a simmer and add the potatoes; that way they keep their shape and trap the flavor."

"Wise owl!"

"Yes, madam."

"Nothing less than alchemy. A sorceress after all."

"It's nothing, madam."

"Soraya..."

Here it comes. I pick up a wooden spoon and make a show of turning over the thick reddish-brown gravy in the pot. It needs water. I pour in a little from the pitcher. When I reach for the salt, she catches my eye. She knows that I'm not going to make this easy for her. This makes her cross, gives her the push to say, quickly, firmly, in a rush, "Soraya, I've decided that I can't have you going home every fortnight anymore. I've spoken to my friends about it, and they're of one mind: that it's not right for me to be left alone so frequently. At my age—don't forget I am more than a decade older than your mother!—anything could happen, I could fall or take ill suddenly, or someone could be watching the house, just waiting for me to be vulnerable. Besides, with Master Timothy's visit coming up we need all hands on deck. Your endless back-and-forth to the Quarter disrupts the rhythm so, and though I've not mentioned it before in deference to your feelings, you're often very absent-minded when you return. Come that Monday, it takes an age for you to settle. Really, this is the only way."

Midway through her little speech, I put down the saltcellar, feeling sentences form in my mouth only for them to stop at my lips.

"I know. I *know*." Her voice is full of kindness. "You've grown used to seeing your family every two weeks. In fact, I blame myself; I try to do what's best for everyone else and it's always at my own expense. For now, you need to stay on until the Christmas break."

"Madam, you've already postponed my visits home twice. I need to see my parents."

She leans back, her eyes slits. "That's very selfish of you, my dear. From what I have gathered, what your parents need is for you to earn a steady wage."

"I have to help my mother—"

"Now don't *fib*, Soraya. You mother has daughters by the dozen. They don't suddenly evaporate come the weekend." She gives an inviting little laugh, but when she realizes that I'm not going to join her, she turns her palms up as though she's out of options. "If you feel you can't manage it, I'm afraid I'll have to find someone else."

There it is. She knows I cannot afford to lose this position. She knows the wage is good and the location—so close to home, so *close!*—means everything. She knows my mother has not been well and I am about to remind her of just this when she says, "Stop *looking* at me like that. I've done so *much* for you. When I think of the *hours* I spend writing your letters to Nour. Name another employer who would take such care of her servant's love ties? Well? It's not him? *What* then? You are concerned about your mother's health? Yes? *Yes*. I thought so. All right. I will allow you to take off one Sunday afternoon a month until Christmas, but we'll need to reassess once Master Timothy is here. You see? I always try to do what is fair, even when it costs me. Please don't look so downcast, my dear—I can't bear it! If something happens at home, one of your siblings could be here in a matter of minutes. Yes? *Good*. Then it's decided."

As she turns to leave, I muster just one question, and in reply, her voice becomes sharp, her back very straight: "A raise? Goodness. That's rather grabbing, my dear. No, there will be no increase in your wage. You'll still be sleeping in my house, eating my food. If anything, I should be *docking* your pay. A matter of counting one's blessings, I should think."

I'm alone for just a moment or two when Fatima arrives, swirls past me and swings first open then shut the cupboard door where the rat poison is kept.

No, I tell her, waving her away. She shrugs one see-through shoulder, her neck growing longer than ever until her head touches the ceiling, before leaving out the back door, across the garden, disappearing as she nears the lemon tree.

I turn back to the pot, ladle out a portion of food for myself for tonight into one bowl and another for tomorrow and set both aside. Then I take a touch of black pepper, insert my finger into my nose and work up a sneeze. I also hawk as much spit and phlegm as I can muster from the back of my throat.

All goes into the pot.

Bon appétit, madam.

It's not that I'm a prisoner here, and to describe myself thus would give my mother cause to say I am once again "telling stories." I can take walks around the neighborhood, I can run her errands, go to the grocer as needs be, carry messages from Mrs. Hattingh to her friends, but I cannot go to the District—*There's no need, my dear. And anyway, on reflection, I should never have let you go there in the first place. A single girl wandering that disreputable place alone? Whatever would your parents think?* I cannot go to the Quarter even for a few hours—*We've so much to* do *here in preparation for Master Timothy's visit, and I know your mother would want you to do it all* well—or down to the parade to buy ribbons and buttons—*It's close by, I know, but again, the time it takes. Best to stay here. You may pick a selection from my own little haberdashery!*

So, I am at Heron Place, day and night.

At first, I do not feel too bad. I busy myself with cleaning what remains of her silver, I shore up things to tell my family, I make secret notes on bits of paper I have collected to remind myself of what to say to Nour during the writing hour, I replay the memory of our kisses and hold myself tight as a happy heat spreads across my face and through me. I tell myself a month is not so long. I tell myself to remain grateful for this job, for gratitude is the salve, gratitude is dignity, gratitude keeps me going. Gratitude keeps me staying.

But by the end of the second week, my longing, my worry for my kin, is strong. My mind turns again and again to how tired Mama has been, how slowly she has begun to move, how rough her hands have turned and how sparingly she uses her oil on them. I think on how Lia will, despite what they say, despite what they hope, soon be sent out to work, and in a few years, so will Alma. Nour will be home this week and I will not see him, for she has refused my request that he be allowed to visit me. "Come *here*? Out of the question. Think, my dear, about what I already do for you and your affianced."

In my loneliness I seek out Rosa and talk to her as I clean Mrs. Hattingh's bedroom. I complain to her, confide in her, and she answers back, mocking madam: *"More than kisses, letters mingle souls."*

I am not supposed to work on a Sunday—it is, after all, their Sabbath—but Mrs. Hattingh wends her way around this by asking me to do a few *small bits, here and there*, since she is *feeling poorly*, and says with a little laugh that since I am not Christian, we're not breaking any commandments.

In the third week I find that I cannot sleep for anger, and nightly I lie wide-eyed, alert, furious in the dark, dreading the day ahead. When I am doing ordinary things—scrubbing at stained linen or peeling potatoes—I have the most terrible thoughts. I wonder, for instance, what would happen if she tripped down the stairs, falling in a heap at the bottom, her neck twisted to the side, still as a doll. I imagine, as I boil a pot of water, that it floats up into the air and empties itself onto her head.

I ignore Fatima, who, as each of these thoughts appears, glides into view and strolls past me, leaving a thin trail of ash in her wake.

I do what I can to stop these thoughts, for they are sinful, wicked, and though a thought is not a deed, it is not without power. *Come, stories,* I plead through gritted teeth, *steal into my mind, banish these ugly, harmful dreams.* But nothing comes; it never does when you ask it to.

I keep busy: I weed the vegetable patch and stop asking Mrs. Hattingh when she'll next have a gardener in.

I move Master Timothy's heavy-as-hell dresser by myself and clean behind it.

I take down the curtains not only to wash but also to mend them.

I stuff newspaper into the window frames to spare her the humiliation of having to do so and myself the punishment that would come if I didn't.

I count up Master Timothy's clothing and notice that a jumper is missing, and when I tell her about it, she beams and says she's sent it over to him in London as a little joke and how good, how *very good*, of me to have noticed and come to her. *Such attention to detail, Soraya!*

I become adept at crochet; under Mrs. Hattingh's watchful eye, I make a dozen little bonnets for her orphan babies' charity.

I clean and clean, but when my mind is still not scrubbed of the bad thoughts, I turn to the job that's at once mindless and tiring: churning butter on her old-fashioned barrel and wheel. Dream-work, this, the beat of churn—*thwack, thwack, thwack*—against the milk. Travel-work. See how I pitch myself far from this house. Look, I'm back in the Quarter. Am I dreaming or remembering? Walking, walking. Evening time, but the heat of the day still with us, the air a soft shawl, Nour beside me. We pass the men coming home from work, the children playing in between the shadows and light cast by the street lanterns. He says, *Tell me one of your stories. Start just as you used to. What was it you'd say?* "This is a story about Good and Evil—"

A story about the Cape, I say, then together: *Names and addresses have been changed to protect reputations.*

That's it. That's it.

And now we are no longer in the street, but standing together on the hilltop, our feet bare, a dassie rustling in the long brush. *Go on.*

Look, Nour says, *we are almost at your home.*

Come. If we stand there, no there . . . by the hibiscus tree. My mother won't see us from there. We race from the hilltop across the street and draw against a wall, hiding beneath the tree that tilts from a neighbor's front garden into the dark of a lampless alleyway. There are ears all around, but at least my mother cannot see us. I lean in close to Nour, drop my voice to a whisper: *All right. Listen. I will tell you everything.*

"Soraya!"

I jump.

"*Soraya!* I've been calling and calling. The butcher's at the door. Tell him I will stop by next week. Tell him I'm poorly. *Hurry.*"

"Yes, madam," I say, the lie ready in my mouth.

* * *

"Did he say when he's coming back?"

"Yes, madam. A week from tomorrow."

"All right."

I don't know where to look. She has called me up to her room, but the state of her! It's midday, but she's changed into her dressing gown and she's sitting on her bed's edge, bold as you please, with the gown slipping down her shoulders, just a silk camisole with thin straps beneath it. No brassiere, so her breasts hang heavy, nipples visible beneath the fabric. I have never seen so much of her. If she feels any shame, it doesn't show. She holds up a small tub of cream, plaintive-like: "I've pulled something. I'm in utter agony. Here. Rub this on my neck."

I glance first at Rosa, who looks as though she's about to explode with laughter, and then tell Mrs. Hattingh, "I don't know how," and also, "What if I make it worse?"

"*Heavens*, Soraya, I need you to apply some ointment, not perform major surgery."

She flips down the camisole strap, turns her head away from me and traces a path with her finger from her hairline to the tip of her shoulder, saying, "Massage from here to here. But wash your hands first. There's some water in my basin."

Moments later I find myself touching her bare skin, looking at the spray of freckles scattering the length of her neck, at the large moles that dot her spine. She's a blusher, I've always known that; her cheeks bloom hot when she's angry. At my touch, her flesh grows pink, first where my fingers have pressed, then like a rash it spreads, brighter and brighter. At this rate, she'll come out in hives, her skin may even blister and weep. I stop. "Is it sore, madam?"

"No, no, this is too wonderful."

And *she'll* say when to stop, thank you very much. Timothy used to do this for her, right up until he left. No, really, I'm far too skilled for this to be the first time.

"It's nothing, madam."

"Clever hands, Soraya. Such strong, clever hands."

"Thank you, madam."

"That'll certainly stand you in good stead when you're married," and she gives a loose laugh.

I keep on, pressing my fingers into her flesh, working away at bumps and knots, while she sighs and shifts.

"Nour's a lucky man," she says dreamily, reaching up to pat my hand, then clamping down on it tight. My hand flinches into a claw beneath hers. "Ow!" she yelps, and turns around, furious. "You scratched me."

I didn't mean to, I tell her, I'll be more careful. But she's decided she's had enough, pulls up her gown and says she'll take supper in her room tonight, something light, scrambled on toast.

I'm at the door when she calls out, "Soraya, lift your hands to your nose. Inhale deeply. Isn't it glorious? Eucalyptus oil in the cream. Masseuse's treat."

That night I dream about her body lined up flat as a door against Nour, her mouth frantic across his face. She bites and kisses everything: mouth, nose, eyes, cheeks, his jawbones, the small dip in the center of his chin. Her hands clutch at his head, and she traces too the outline of his ears, all the while whimpering, "Dear boy, dear boy."

TWELVE

"I believe I could get a very nice little sum for her in London," says the thin man.

This day has been full of surprises.

It began with Mrs. Hattingh calling to me, as if in great distress, from her bedroom. I raced up the stairs to find her at the fireplace, standing on a chair, one foot on each of its arms, struggling under Rosa.

"*Help!*"

I lunged forward just as the edge of the gilt frame was about to slide past her knees and hit the floor.

"The *weight* of this thing! You've no notion!"

"Yes, madam."

She'd forgotten, apparently, that one of her never-to-be-broken instructions is that Rosa's frame must be cleaned once a month and that I lower it, alone, to do just that.

When both were safely on the ground, Mrs. Hattingh brushed

down her skirt and said, "We need to carry her downstairs. She's to be in the drawing room today; I'm having someone over to assess her."

I didn't know what she was talking about.

An hour later there was a knock at the door. There stood a stranger to me, a thin-waisted man with a small, pointed beard and poky eyes in an old-fashioned frock coat and hat. He clicked closed a smart pocket watch and said to let Mrs. Hattingh know that Mr. Samuel Avery was here. It was clear from the way he strode in that he was familiar with 23 Heron Place, and when Mrs. Hattingh emerged from the drawing room to greet him in the passageway in her usual way, hands thrust before her, a welcome cry on her lips, he responded by kissing her hand. She giggled as he told her how well she looks, and he asked about Master Timothy and, as ever, she was like a windup doll with this question, and all we heard for the next five minutes was about her boy's goings-on in London. Mr. Avery stood captive in the hallway, gasping in wonderment at each new piece of information—where Master Timothy lives! what he does!—and only when Mrs. Hattingh stopped to catch her breath did he offer quietly, "What a mercy he was spared," to which she agreed, casting her eyes upward, as though she were *even now* thanking her Maker. Then she ushered him to the drawing room and I followed. When he caught sight of Rosa he said how "exquisite" she was, he's always thought so, and how, if Mrs. Hattingh was willing, he could take her up to London with him on his next voyage—just a month from now!—it would make the sale so much better.

That's when I realize he's here to tell madam how much Rosa could be worth—she must be having even more money troubles than I thought. As Mr. Avery speaks, I understand he sold the other paintings too, because he says things like, "I've heard that

Omar has changed hands a number of times over the years, but the Featherstones are determined to build their family collection, so Apollo, the flower seller and the seamstress have stayed on in Bucklebury. *Bucklebury!* Of all places."

Mrs. Hattingh is smiling as though her life depends on it and says it gives her unmatched pleasure to know they're in such good homes, with people who understand their worth, and Mr. Avery responds that he quite agrees, and either he doesn't notice the way the side of her jaw is pulsing or he pretends not to.

"Now, whether or not we find her a buyer, I'd like to meet up with Timothy again. I've not seen him since he signed up. And at Langridge's in the City, you say? I'd be glad to take up a few things from home if you like? I assure you, it would be no trouble. A small gesture for one of our very own heroes."

Mrs. Hattingh says how wonderful that would be, only Timothy's always so busy, they work him such terrible hours; also, she believes he's going on a little holiday at that time, traveling on the Continent with his young lady before he makes his way down to see his old mother. She *thinks* there'll be an announcement soon—at this they both give a knowing laugh—but, of course, she doesn't dare press him on it. If anything, Mr. Avery could bring something back *for her.*

"At your service," he replies.

"A newspaper."

Another shared laugh, and back and forth they go about how "grim" the standard of writing is in the local papers, how impossible it is to keep up with the arts from here.

I stop listening to them after a while. This is the first I've heard about Master Timothy spending any time away from London, and it's curious she's never mentioned it to me because she tells me every bit of news she gets from him. Maybe she didn't want to say he'd be going away with this girl when they're not even married. I'd be ashamed of that too. She won't even let Nour visit me, she tells me to watch what I say in the letters to him, but there's her son traipsing about all over the world out of wedlock. If I did that my parents would say I was taking the skin off their faces. What a family this is! She's still going on about the "quality" of the papers when Mr. Avery walks over to Rosa, saying, "Really, she grows more lovely as the years pass." Then he leans in: "To business!"

He's almost on top of her now, those small eyes trailing over her skin, his breath on her shawl. Rosa can smell him, I should think; it's too close, too close, and when I glance over I see Mrs. Hattingh, like me, give a little flinch on Rosa's behalf.

Madam decides this is a good moment to send me out to get the tea, and when I return, she is sitting down, looking deliberately away from the painting and directly at him. "It will be a blow to let go of my Rosa, Mr. Avery. She is my company."

"It is *agony* to part with those we love."

"Mr. Hattingh was the art collector, but I was always the art *admirer*."

"Quite so, quite so. I hope I can find a just sum that ameliorates the loss."

Mrs. Hattingh's shoulders droop, and she declares that no sum, *no sum*, could *ever* make up for losing Rosa, but when Mr. Avery names one, she straightens a little and says that though it doesn't bear thinking about, she will have to summon the courage.

The number is more than seven times my annual wage. It seems impossible. How could Rosa fetch such a sum? She doesn't *do* anything. She's just *there*. On the wall. My every day, my every hour, for more than seven years is worth less to these people than a picture. I don't care if Rosa is looking at me now in her glancing way, full of sorrowful apology: *It's not my fault,* she seems to say.

I've not said a word, but my feelings must have filled the room, because Mrs. Hattingh says, "That will be all, Soraya."

She's always like this when she has guests—either she grows more formal in her tone or she behaves as though I've disappeared, melded with the furniture.

As I leave, Mr. Avery says, "Now *she* has a tremendous face. Unusually long neck too. I wonder if she'd consider sitting for Brookes. He pays rather well."

"Now, now, don't you pinch her from me."

"I wouldn't dream of it." A laugh, and then, thoughtfully, "Curious how very like Rosa she looks."

"It's uncanny, isn't it? Both from the Quarter. I daresay they're related. Well, there's the upside: if I'm missing Rosa too much, I can just look over at Soraya."

Their laughter runs down the hallway.

In the kitchen I drink a glass of water. Anything to singe the burning in my chest. I can't say what has made me angrier: that they are going to sell her—No, not *her*, I tell myself, *it. It.*—or that *it* is worth so very much more than I am. I pour another glass for Fatima, who stands beside me, her body aglow with rage.

It is only by chance that I see the letter from Nour first. I am in the front garden, sweeping the path free of the night's fallen olive leaves, when the postman arrives early. Usually, Mrs. Hattingh positions herself at the gate, receives all correspondence and lets me know if Nour has written. As his letter is placed into my hands, my shoulders go slack and a slow creep of heat rises through my legs, and I feel *joy*, a whole handful of it. I run back toward the house and directly into Mrs. Hattingh. Caution forgotten, I wave the envelope at her: "See here! He has written! He has *written*!" before putting it carefully into my apron pocket. I turn to pick up a bucket—it is lighter than air, and today the floors will wash themselves—when Mrs. Hattingh stops me. "But, my dear," she says, "what if you were to splash water on the paper and damage it?"

I shake my head, my hand goes to my pocket, tightens around the paper, crinkling it, ruining it probably, as she continues.

"It is better, I think, if I keep it for you. I promise that we will read it together tonight and write him back. Come now, hand it over. I will keep it safe."

She puts out one hand, palm up, fingers together, and calls the letter to her.

I walk after her to see where she will put it. It's all I can do not to say, *I can read the damn thing perfectly well* myself! because I can already hear her response: *How very untrustworthy you've turned out to be. What-else-have-you-lied-about? After-everything-I-have-done-for-you.*

From the drawing room door, I watch as she lays the letter on her desk, stroking two fingers back and forth over my name. When she looks up, she's surprised to see me.

"What is it? Why are you in here? Go on . . . back to work with you. Honestly, I give you an inch."

In the kitchen I reach for Mrs. Hattingh's mother's willow-patterned sugar bowl.

I'll tell her it just *slipped* from my hands—*Just so, madam, I can't think what happened*—even as I drop it to the floor.

The crash calls Mrs. Hattingh.

"Honestly, Soraya," Mrs. Hattingh scolds, "I've told you time and time again to be careful. Of all my dishes! Anyone else would take it out of your wages. You'd have to work a year to pay it off!"

She looks down sadly at the feathery blue-and-white shards.

"You are so distracted lately. I think the letter writing has been altogether too much for you. Perhaps we should stop."

"No!" I cry out.

"You see? This is precisely what I mean. You are so excitable. It cannot be good for you."

She is so calm when she says this. Calmer even than when she took away my visits home. *Look at her,* I think, look how easily she can gift and punish. Look how it's nothing to her, nothing to snatch back what brings me joy and consolation, what is *mine*, especially now when every day moves at a crawl. I realize I will have to beg. Make myself small so she can be big. *That's the trick, my girl,* my mother would have said, *stoop low so they can feel tall.*

"I'm sorry, Mrs. Hattingh. It was an accident. I'll be more careful. *Please*, we must keep writing the letters."

I keep my hands clenched at my sides, so angry I could explode, but I work up a few tears to disguise the rage. Though she delivered the threat with ease, Mrs. Hattingh is unprepared for my face: it's twisted as I pretend to make every effort not to cry. Alarmed, she reaches to touch my cheek, traces a hand over my head, cups my chin and says soothingly, "All right. All right. Calm yourself, my girl. We'll keep writing. We will keep the hour. But a whole day's labor stretches before you. Mind you get through everything. I trust nothing else will be broken."

She walks away, her slight frame straight, arms soft and graceful, once a girl who would have practiced with a book on her head, and I marvel that she can so easily show me her back when the kitchen is full of knives.

*   *   *

She calls me to her drawing room—bell ringing, "*Soraya, Soraya, Soraya*"—and I see that she has placed on the table between us Nour's letter.

"Come now. Sit yourself down, my girl."

"Does madam want to read my letter now?"

"Goodness! What a question. It's not a matter of *my* wishes. I don't do this for *me*. I said to *sit*, my dear. We'll forget the unpleasantness of this morning. Let's see how Nour is getting on."

"Yes, madam."

I take my seat, hold myself very still and fold my hands in my lap; she will not see my nails cutting into my palms.

Knife in hand, she slits the envelope open.

Dear Soraya,

I should begin with the weather, shouldn't I? I should tell you that the nights grow warmer and the days longer . . .

As she reads, I realize something: I'd always known that when I speak and she writes, she takes my "I," but today I realize when she reads, she takes Nour's too.

Dimly, I can hear her describe his difficulties: time, his wage, *it's impossible to save anything*, his sister's wedding, his mother's health. I seem to be leaving this room. It is too painful to stay here, impossible to remain, a kind of torture to hear Nour's voice through hers, to listen to him—her—speak about our people, our lives. Easier to let my senses be taken with what is happening outside. It is nearly dusk's end, night gathers close, in a few hours the stars will fill the sky, the month's half-moon will appear, the smell of jasmine—lush and sweet—will deepen at the windowsill and the crickets will begin their awful, endless song. It's a still, still evening in which every sound carries, and I can hear, streets away, the creak of a wagon wheel and the *clop-clop-clop* of its horse. Drifting. I must pull myself together, come back to this room. It is so difficult. Everything is difficult and has been for so long. I tilt my head, telling myself, *Try, try*, and I listen more carefully to Mrs. Hattingh's beautiful reading voice, which has changed, suddenly, into one of concern. "Goodness. That's bad luck isn't it, Soraya?"

"Madam?"

"Nour losing his place at the Teachers Training College . . . what a setback."

My stomach skitters to my feet, my mouth turns dry. I shake my head, no, no, it cannot be so.

"Poor thing. Here, I'll read it again: 'The college does not have a place for me this year. But they say I may try again next year.' Now don't look so *glum*, my dear. The months will fly by, and it may be for the best. Nour can save a little more, and I promise to keep you busy. We've a mountain of books to get through! What else does he have to say? Ah, bless. He's ever steadfast and optimistic."

I listen, stone faced, to his talk about the studies he remains sure are to come, the job that will be offered, the wedding that will be celebrated, our life and golden future ahead. I am the storyteller, I think, but Nour is the bearer of hope, foolish hope, unreasonable hope, *stupid* hope. A wedding in a year! What a fantasy. Likely, I will be ancient, a hag by the time any of this happens, still working at Mrs. Hattingh's, our hair a matching gray, our gaits matching stoops, *part of the family, part of the furniture, comes with the house.*

Then I remember Mrs. Hattingh's friendship with the important man at the college and her offer once to speak to him about Nour.

"Madam. That man, that one from the school, the college, the one you know."

"Mr. Cartwright? Capital fellow."

"Can you ask Mr. Cartwright to help? To give Nour his place back for this year?"

"That's an idea! I I tend to think it's not good form to question decisions already made—heaven knows they have their own reasons and it may jeopardize his next application—but let's see . . . I'll go on, shall I? Goodness, I'm suddenly quite tired. It's been a long day, but I'll persevere. Tomorrow we'll write Nour a reassuring response telling him you don't mind waiting. Not a bit."

I nod dully, another year unfurling before me.

"'I received the jumper. It fits! Please thank Mrs. Hattingh—' Really, Soraya. Tell him to think nothing of it!"

What jumper?

"'I look quite smart in it . . .' I bet he does!"

Say something.

"I hoped they'd be about the same height and weight, but you never know. Really, nutrition is everything—"

"I didn't know about a jumper, madam."

"What's that?"

"The jumper, madam. I didn't know you sent it to Nour—"

"Oh! Didn't I mention it? I sent him one of Lieutenant Hattingh's old ones. He won't mind—always generous to a fault, my son. And Nour's complained about the cold more than once. I'm sure I told you. In fact, it was *you* who noticed it was gone."

"Yes, madam, you said you sent it to Master Timothy."

"Did I? Well, if you say so."

Fatima appears just behind me, urging me to look at the circle of ash floating and whirling around Mrs. Hattingh's head: *Say something more,* she whispers.

"You said . . . you said you sent it to him as a joke . . ."

She ignores me, returning to the letter, eyes on the page, nodding, smiling at something else Nour has said.

"Madam? I don't understand—"

"I'm sorry. *What* is it you're asking me?"

"About the jumper, madam. You said . . . you said you sent it to Master Timothy and now you're saying you sent it to Nour."

She brings the letter to the table, places one hand over another and stares out as though greatly offended. Then she takes the pages and folds them over, places them back into the envelope, makes a great show of opening one of her writing desk's little drawers, placing the letter inside and locking it with a tiny key. "I'm going to bed. Mind you choke the fire," she says as she leaves the room.

In the weeks that follow, Mrs. Hattingh is distant, she doesn't stop by the kitchen as often as usual, she passes me in the hallway without comment. She does pen the promised reassuring reply to Nour that the delay in getting to the college is a challenge—*nothing more!*—and then jokes to me that she "daren't" suggest writing to him again, seeing the fuss I make about everything. I just stare at her until I see, clear as day, Nour, standing before me, face bloody, arm half gone, wearing her son's jumper. I shake my head to clear the vision and calm my heart. Foolishness.

She spends the next weeks rushing from committee meeting to tea party to jamboree, and we seldom speak about anything apart from the house, and even then, she lets some tasks slip; there are fewer instructions and inspections, and I let the dust linger on the windowsills. There is one thing that she remains unmoved about: my going before the month is out. *No,* she says when I try to bring it up. *No. I need you here. To prepare.*

Weeks pass, and I do not hear from Nour. At first, I thought she might be keeping his correspondence from me, so I waited one morning for the postman and asked him directly. A kind man, he smiled, told me that there's been no response to that last letter sent from Heron Place a month ago, but, with a knowing nod to the house and my employer, to keep checking with him.

Never mind her, I think, dully. What about Nour? Why has he not written? We told him that I didn't mind about the college. Why has he not sent a single message?

THIRTEEN

I am in the garden, bent over a bucket, wringing out Mrs. Hattingh's stockings, when Kashif comes charging toward me, panting at animal speed. It is a shock to see him—almost two months have passed since I was allowed home, and he has, I swear, grown four inches. He must have let himself in through the side gate, because there is no sign of madam.

"What are you doing here? Is it Mama? Is she sick? *Speak!*"

Kashif shakes his head, eyes red, mouth pressed tight, and then just one word before he breaks into a wail: "Papa."

My father.

Our father, Kashif cries, has been ill for weeks, in bed, wheezing, tired, the weight dropping off him, his qalam pen unused, the ink neglected and left to dry out. And in the last two days, slipping further away, telling my mother about those who stand at the edge of his bed, waiting, waiting, *See how they wait?* The imam has come, and Mama has been praying all night at his bedside. Kashif's words rush and roar and swirl all around, but somehow I wring out the last of the water from the tangled stocking legs and hang them up to dry. I tug off my apron and walk to my room, where I change my headscarf. In the house, Kashif trails after me, eyes wide, staring, staring at it all: the height of the ceilings, the length of the passageway, the richness of it *still* despite Mrs. Hattingh's losses. I find her and tell her I am going home and why. Her hand travels fast to her mouth, and in the midst of my rising worry, I feel relief when she says, "Of course, go. *Go*. Your poor mother."

We run across town, me faster than Kashif, for he is exhausted from his race to Mrs. Hattingh's. But he tries to keep up, telling me over and over that he's "sorry, sorry," he would have come sooner, told me sooner, but Mama forbade it, everyone was worried about me keeping my job. Especially now when Mama is so tired.

We run down hills and then up them, across the length of the dipped bowl of the city. *Papa*. We dart past carriages, and I don't make way for settler men. *Papa*. I don't care that the hem of my skirt turns filthy, that my feet are burning in these too-tight shoes or that my chest is sore, wheezing, because we must run, we must run. As we turn the corner to our street, the three trees come into view—hibiscus, loquat, lemon—and also a crush of people who are around the house, and oh no, *oh no, Papa*, why are they here already and why is the smell of incense so close and who is that auntie walking toward the house, her steps slow and heavy, her arms full of roses? Kashif and I keep running, keep running, until we are at the gate, pushing past people who say to one another, "They are here, look, they are here!" and down the small passageway to my parents' bedroom, where my sisters stand weeping, then turn and raise their hands to me, "Come, come," and into the room Kashif and I go, and there is my mother, bent over my father, her whole body shaking, and another auntie stroking her shoulders, saying, "Inna lillahi wa inna ilayhi raji'un" *To Him we belong and to Him we must return*, and there is my father, still and small, arms folded across his chest, his head already bound so that his jaw doesn't fall slack, and it's all I can do not to reach out and stop them because it cannot be so, it cannot be so, and I'm sure that if I can stop everyone from behaving as though he is gone, I can put an end to this foolishness, because it cannot be so. He was fine, *fine*, that's all Mama ever told me, that he was fine. I want to scream, and for a moment I am sure that I am screaming, but no, I'm silent. A woman hands me a tasbih, and another's voice calls, gently, gently, from the doorway that we must make way, the men are here, they have come, they are here to wash the body.

My mother does not care who sees her, she smokes her secret pipe in the open and says yes to whatever calming medicine is placed into her hands. My sisters and I walk through the house like spirits; we are in our longest dresses, our scarves locked tight against our chins. We can say nothing but what we are meant to say: *Inna lillahi wa inna ilayhi raji'un.*

People are smaller in death, even if death is just a few hours old. "It is the soul departing the body that makes it so," says my aunt as she drapes the hallway mirror with a sheet and then turns to wipe the kohl from my eyes. "None of that today, child."

My father's body is before me, wrapped in white cloth, pressed with rose petals, camphor rising like a strong note in an unwanted song. My uncles lay my father out in the front room; they surround their brother, raise their hands, weep for him, pray for him. Then our people come. There is not space enough in the house for them, so they line the streets, for Papa was loved, and we of the Quarter know one another home and hearth. One by one they bend to kiss his forehead, hold us mourners close, offer more prayers.

It is too much, the feeling dark and loamy, a hole in my stomach, an ache in my heart, the swirl of people, and my father, me, my father, me, being held by too many, kissed by too many.

And in all the people who come, one is absent.

Where is Nour? He should have been here from early light, should have been among the first to kiss my mother's hand, kneel at her feet, assure her that she is his mother too, to hug my sisters, tell my little brother that he will wash our father's body alongside him. He should be here now to hoist my father's bier onto his shoulder, carry him out of the house and to the mosque, stand tightly next to the men at funeral prayers, one body, one aching heart, one plea for the soul who is returning. He should be at my father's grave, helping to dig it, using his hands if he has no shovel. He should be scattering rose petals on the earth before lowering my father into the ground, in that patch of land high above our neighborhood, burying him with our family and our leaders, every one of their graves pointing toward our holy city.

Where is he? *Where is he?*

In the kitchen the women cook and weep.

To Him we belong and to Him we must return.

Grief has spread itself wide and deep over our house. Children sit quiet on the steps between our stoep and the street.

In the days ahead, my mother and siblings and I keep strange hours; we light candles at two, three, four o'clock in the morning, because there is neither refuge in sleep nor comfort in the dark. We are newly thin, food tastes of little and flesh falls from our bodies. We sleep in one bed. When we look at others, we are both here and not here, because we are always on the lookout. We are waiting, you see, for him to come back.

There is a path, not too far from the cannon, that winds around the hill. It is rough with rocks and crushed stones that crunch underfoot. In the spring, all around, white and yellow daisies blink back at the sun and the air carries the smoky, earthy smell of our fine bushes in bloom. The hill dips steeply down, and the sensation of wanting to run, run, *run* right off the path's edge takes me. When I was a child I would climb onto a rock, tilt myself forward, wave my arms, pretend first at flailing, then falling down into the porcelain blue of the ocean below.

It was there, beneath the water, that I first found the seawoman with her blood-ink and her terrible kisses, and later, others: a child curled like a snail against her father, him still chained to the wreck of a ship; a wooden chest covered in sea flowers, and locked tight within each petal a drowned one's soul. Once, I saw a woman sit smiling and nodding beside a giant loom. Her robes floated up as she spun and spun just one thing, a single golden thread, that traveled all the way from that watery floor to the land and then up into the Quarter, where it wove itself around each of our homes, stitching us forever to the ocean and to one another.

Both my mother and father brought me here, my mother to gather plants and herbs—*Here, Soraya, here's the sour fig, there's the buchu, behind that rock is rooibos*—and she would touch each fruit or leaf lightly, testing its readiness before she plucked it. My father would say, as he stared out at the glittering water, *It is difficult to remember all we have lost at sea.*

What did he mean by that? Too late, I realize, an ache washing over me, to ask him now.

It has been six days since Papa's funeral, and I have come up here for a moment's solitude. Tomorrow I must return to Heron Place, and the thought of it is a small stone in my chest. I have run from the busyness of a grieving house with its endless stream of visitors and nightly prayers that have gone on all this first week, from the sympathy that feels like claiming: *Your father did this for me. Your father meant that to me.*

They mean well, my mother says, but I do not want to hear from anyone who is not her or a sibling about the days before he died: *I just saw him now-now, the other day, just last week, and we never knew, we never knew, but shame he didn't look himself.* I do not want to hear because it is unbearable that they saw him in his final days, but I did not.

I do not want to look at his friends or brothers or anyone his age or older, because I only wonder, my heart bursting with aching fury as I look, why *they* are still here, and he is not.

Nour, I have not heard from. His mother said very little to me when I saw her, only that Nour was sorry, he'd received word about the funeral late, that there was no point in racing home because my father would be long buried by the time he'd gotten here, but that he would return to greet my mother next week. She looked shamed—as well she might—and I slipped off as soon as I could, saying my mother needed me.

This morning I'd woken hours before the sun, even before first prayers, had crept out of bed, pulled the sheet back over my sisters, smoothed out Lia's hair lying thick and tangled across her face. On the stoep, I looked up at the crescent moon and then out onto the starlit street, and in that thick quiet, I wept for my father and raged that Nour had abandoned me to this.

As soon as it was daybreak, I'd woken my mother and told her I was going for a walk. And I came to this place where I used to gather my friends, the Quarter's children, to hear my stories and sometimes, for a precious hour, with my father. *Let us go and greet the Lion*, he would say, meaning both the secretive animals that roamed this mountain and the great rock shaped like one. And each time, once we reached the cannon, he would turn silent and stare out at the coast.

Mostly, my father walked here alone. He wanted what I have now: the quiet of my own thoughts, the chance to notice everything without interruption, to take deep breaths of earth and dry bush, to see the birds circling, to hear the dassies scuttle.

If I squint a little, I can see myself, seven years old, standing at our front-room window, barefoot in a cotton dress, watching my father's thin ankles peek out from his wide-legged trousers, smelling the smoke that curled from his pipe and over his shoulder as he set off.

These last years, he did not go walking as frequently, and if his legs were weak and his breath short, I'd refused to see it. When asked about his health, I told people stoutly that he was strong as an ox. If I said it enough times, it would be so.

I look at my hands: in the last months they've grown rough with all that cleaning, scrubbing, soaking. They're like my mother's now, my fingers thickening and knotting before my eyes. They will never, I realize, be ink stained like Papa's, will never write prayers that hold God's messages.

How often I used to steal into his room to watch him work, to see him sitting at his table, paper and qalam at the ready, head in his hand, a night's devotion behind him, a day's cursive ahead of him, the window opened to let in the air and the angels. I'd tiptoe to his side, and he would put an arm out, call me to him, show me the text, sacred and sure—*See how my hand holds the pen? See how the words flow right to left?*—tell me to put a saucer of milk out for the neighborhood cats who'd congregate just outside and smile, eyes crinkling, when we heard Mama calling, and I'd dive to hide under his table: *Soraya! Soraya! Where's that child gone now?*

"Mama sent me. She says you must come back."

I know without turning that it's Kashif.

"Why? What task needs doing?"

"I don't know. Just come."

"Tell her I'll be there soon."

"Must I wait with you?"

He reaches for my hand, and I think it's because he wants to try to lead me home, but he just stands there, holding it, looking at me with big eyes.

"Is it true you're going back to work tomorrow?"

"I am."

"Do you like it there by her?"

He's so soft, Kashif. Seven years younger than me, a child still.

"No one *likes* their work. How would you like to be away from home all the time?"

At this, he looks set to cry, and I realize he's worried about being sent away too. "Don't be scared for nothing, man! You and the girls aren't going anywhere."

He blinks. "Do you know who's going to get Papa's job?"

"Not *you*." I can't help it; my laugh sounds like a bark. "Not with those thick fingers."

"I never evens said I wanted it!"

"Papa didn't train anyone to come after him, so I don't know. Come. Come stand here. Do you see that?"

"What?"

"The Lion—"

"*What?! Where?!*"

"No, man. The shape of that rock there is a lion."

But Kashif has Mama's eyes; a rock is a rock. We lean against the same boulder, and an easy silence grows between us until he breaks it, saying, "People are saying there's something wrong with you."

"What are you talking about?"

"Because no one's seen you cry for Papa. And that that's also why Nour is staying away from you. Because you're strange from your job."

"*Who* said that?!"

"I don't know. A lot of people."

"A lot of people don't know what they're talking about."

"I'm just telling you what I hear. I didn't know what to tell them."

"Tell them to mind their own side of the street."

"But . . ."

"But *what*?"

"I . . . I—"

"I. I. I," I mock him. "What's that? A stutter for an excuse? You forgot how to be loyal to your own?"

"I haven't seen you cry either, Raya, and that's not right!"

"Oh, well, if no one has seen it I must not be grieving."

I stalk past him, picking my way fast down the hill's path without any care for the tripping stones or scraping bushes. He is close behind me, urging me to *be careful, please be careful*, but he needn't;

I know this path better than most, and more, I travel it now with our father's knowledge to guide me.

The wind rustles through the tall, dry grass, the sun is hot on my face, the sky a burning blue.

"Raya?" Kashif is weeping. "I'm sorry, I'm sorry for what I said."

I stop, hand him my handkerchief and, without thinking, rub my hand on his back as we walk. "And me," I say.

As we near our house, one of the women standing on her stoep sees us and calls out, "*Soraya*! What's taking you so bladdy long? Hurry up! Your *mother needs you*!"

It's a Sunday, so everyone is out on the street, and they watch as I lead my crying brother inside.

The passageway feels narrower than ever, the walls are close and thick.

My mother calls me from the kitchen. I expect to find her weeping into her rice, but instead she says, "There's a present for you on your father's table."

I wonder where Papa is? That's the first thing I think as I enter his workroom, and I have to stop myself from calling for him, asking my mother if he's out and, if so, when he'll be back. I want only to rush out, anywhere, anywhere, even back to Heron Place.

Stay here, I tell myself. Stand here.

His chair is one his father made for him, the leather worn shiny at the seat, the brass studs that dot its edges in need of a polish. On his table, long and facing the window, are a lattice wooden box containing paper, ink, his pens; a small bowl, inside of which nestles a charcoal disc and burned frankincense; also a packet of tobacco, a small water glass and jug. A tasbih with a maroon tassel hangs on the window handle. I don't know which, if any, of these things my mother wants to make a gift. The tobacco is tempting, but I know my mother will go into a rage, so I pick up the jug, thinking it as good a memento as any. My knees feel suddenly like water. I lean against the wall, and that's when I smell him, as sure as if he were standing right next to me. My throat thickens and I whisper, "*Papa, Papa*," because he is here, right *here*. Already come to visit. *Already.* See how much he loves me, even if Nour doesn't; misses me, even if Nour doesn't; has refused accession, will stay in this realm however long he can—only to realize that the scent is coming from his coat hanging on a hook next to me.

Back in the kitchen I tell my mother I've taken the jug, and she looks over at me, bewildered. "The *jug*? No. No. Come ma, I'll show you what's yours."

I hold my breath—I do not want to smell him again—and follow her.

"Ag, I thought I put it on top of the table." She opens the wooden box—at home in this room she's barely spent time in—and takes out a sheet of paper. "He made this for your and Nour's home. For when you get married."

She holds it up to her chest and tells me, almost shyly, that it was one of the last rakams he did. We look at it together. It's so simply done: the verses have not been shaped into a moon's sliver or a raindrop, there is no adornment or framing pattern. There are only the words, running right to left, only the holy letters—the writing of each, my father used to say, a pathway to the divine, to the great reunion. I look carefully to see if there is any evidence of his hand tiring, his mind slipping—a shaky stroke, a blurred dot—but all is as it should be. He must have been guided, I say eventually to my mother, he must have felt the oneness he always sought.

* * *

I leave home the next day, bound for Mrs. Hattingh's, promising to return as soon as I'm allowed. Mama draws me to her, covers my face with kisses and hands me my father's wooden box. She lifts her chin as though telling me to open it. Inside the box, just as I knew there would be, three of my father's qalams, his small glass inkpot, sheets of rice paper bleached white.

All I can think about is how I am returning to the woman who kept me from my father's bedside, robbed me of our last talks, stole our farewell. *Witch. Thief.* And though I vowed months ago to Mama that I'd keep my anger in check—*Please, Soraya, just please*—the closer I get to Heron Place, the stronger my fury.

Mrs. Hattingh is waiting for me at the gate. She says how sorry she is for my loss, offers her deep condolences and says, "He's in a better place."

"And how is your mother?"

I answer as though from another shore, but my mind is jumping up-down-in-out-all-around. I watch her mouth as she speaks, see her teeth flashing, lips pursing, opening, stretching into a smile, and it's everything I can do not to pull that tongue out until it is several feet long and wrap it around her snake-tight, till her breath's gone for good.

I tell her my mother is managing, madam, thank you, thank you, and yes-yes, I'm very tired, and no, I won't go back till next month, and thank you—thank you for the week's leave, and yes-yes, grief is a painful thing, but I take comfort that he is with his Maker now, and yes-yes, best I go to my room, put my things down and see you in the morning, fires built, tea and toast on tray. My mother's sent more kumquat jam and her thanks, her thanks, her grateful thanks.

She follows me as I make my way through the house, chattering about this and that, how quiet it's been with me away, what she's eaten, how the carpet in Birds needs a good brush and, in between, the same question over and over. Eventually I answer her: "No, madam, Nour wasn't there."

I must be looking at her very curiously, because she stops suddenly and tells me to go to my room, to rest, that I look exhausted, and with a tilt of her head and a voice full of sympathy, "not to worry, really," she'll get her own supper tonight.

Exhausted, yes, but when I do sleep, my dreams give me little rest. I wake up in the deep night to find Fatima more present than ever: this time she lifts the skirt of her dress so that it balloons, whirs in a cloud of air as she crosses the room. She settles down next to me, bringing not her usual ash, but a gray mist of ocean fog, making me shiver and shake with cold. She tells me, as though it is a comfort, that she will not leave my side, that she is sister and mother to me both, and not to mind the madam, not tonight anyway. Then, as though the idea has just come to her, announces, *We must go up the mountain!* and races out the door, through the garden, and climbs up the rocks, nimble as a goat, urging, *Hurry! Follow me.* She leads me to a cave—*This is where we ran to*, she says— and ushers me inside. In the cave's corner a group of our people, their feet bleeding from the trek across stones and crags, eyes wild from fighting baboons and wildcats, cupped hands holding either prayers or water. On the walls, they have scratched the number of days they've hidden out here, drawn a line through every four in the way that prisoners do. I look up; the scratches are endless, uncountable, covering every inch of rock. How is this possible, I ask Fatima, how long have they been here? She laughs and strokes my face: *We are here and in their houses and on their streets and all over the city, and we are the living and the dead, and the dead are us, in us and upon us, generation upon generation, and so we mark our days and the days that stretch behind us and the days that stretch before us, and we ask how many days are in a hundred years? How many thousand days lie ahead?* She draws me toward her and lifts up the branch of a tree, thin and bleached. A trick of light makes its shadow look at once like the antlers of a deer, the curve of the ratib sword and also, I think, my eyes brimming, my father's qalam.

If I am spent, Mrs. Hattingh is full of beans, quicker to laugh, faster to move these days than before. All rests easy on her, whereas my tiredness is bone-deep; I am weighed down, bottomed out, old-woman weary. I struggle to get out of bed. Sleep lies so heavy on me that sometimes I wake thinking that I am in my kafan, already bound tight in the white cotton of my burial shroud. Away from my kin, my father's passing feels like a terrible dream. There is no one here to talk to who knew him, remembers him; no one to share a grief so mighty that I wonder some days how my heart goes on beating. Before I came to this house, I used to get up, quick-quick, from a dream straight into the day, but now there are times when I don't know if I am asleep or in the world. I am thick, slow, cold, and this is what worries me the most, because I have always been one to move. Even in stillness, my body has always carried its own heat. But these mornings my thoughts form as slowly as fabric loosens in the ocean, lazy, drifting. I wake up one morning thinking, *I live underwater.*

The weeks pass, and there is no word—not a letter, not even a message—from Nour, and I waver between worry that something has happened to him and a deep dread that his feelings have changed and he is done with me. When the worry comes, I feel as though my head were on fire. When the dread comes, I want only to lie down, never to wake up again. Perhaps he feels such shame about losing his place at the college that he cannot face me, even now, even over my father's grave. I must tell him that all will be well. I must ask him why he has abandoned me, find out what is going on. He owes me that much.

I gather the energy one day to ask Mrs. Hattingh if we could write to him, and she replies that it wouldn't do to send "love letters" while I am in mourning. As ever, I cannot say what I know: that I will never *not* be in mourning, and anyone who has lost someone would say the same. It's as though she latches on to my thought, because she goes on to say that in fact, even after the mourning period has passed, she would hesitate to make contact because it would be improper to correspond with a young man who has not written to me in so long. "Didn't attend your father's funeral and now incommunicado, just when you need him most. The cruelty of a lover's silence! But there's some good fortune in knowing his true character . . . Gosh, when I think of the evenings spent on our letters—why, I feel quite disappointed too."

But, she continues, she too misses the joy and purpose of our writing hour. Now, now, I mustn't get too excited and think she's going to reinstate it. She has another idea. We will not write, but we will increase our *reading* together. Not weekly, but nightly. She may even spend a little more of that time teaching *me* how. We'll start with her favorite: Dickens. There are passages, she says, eyes shining, of *Little Dorrit* that never fail to move her.

If my hours outside the house had shrunk before my father died, they now amount to nothing. Mrs. Hattingh does not let me leave Heron Place. Not even to run errands. She tells me she'll post my wage directly to my mother. *She must need the money now more than ever, my dear.* We've lost so much time, she explains, with my having gone to the funeral and stayed a whole week. There's still ever so much to *do* ahead of Master Timothy's visit. *No distractions! Think. Just a few more weeks, Soraya!* She may even get me a new uniform if she can stretch to it—she's just seen some very smart ones in the paper.

Also, she's not wanted to mention it before—I've been so gloomy—but best to be clear: it was all right that my brother delivered the message about my father, but she can't have Kashif making a habit of dropping by willy-nilly. If he does, she'll make sure he understands that and send him on his way.

I am not even allowed to wait for the postman, because receiving her son's letters is one of her "chief joys" and she wants to "delight" in every bit of the process, and that includes collecting them. So there is no chance of sending a letter in secret to Nour—though how I'd manage without her noticing an envelope and stamp missing is another worry.

* * *

Each night, she reads to me. I struggle to follow what she's saying, but it doesn't seem to matter; what she wants is for me to listen, to remain in her company until she is ready for bed. I avoid her during the day. Whenever I am with her, whatever strength I've been able to scrape together overnight drains away and my head feels full and empty at the same time. Nour has still not written, not once, and as much as I long to hear from him, I also want to see my mother, my siblings. I need to be with my own. Just this morning as I cleaned the ivory elephant, I was sure its eyes were winking at me, and my father's voice echoed in my mind: *Something that lived once can stay living: trees milled into paper, a bird's feather made into a quill, sheep's hair woven into wool. Things go on, even in death.* At that last word, I dropped to the floor next to the elephant, a wail rising from deep within and, with it, a longing to be held by my father, to walk with him to the Lion, to listen to him, to speak to him. I stopped weeping only because Fatima stood over me, saying sternly, *Don't let her hear you. Don't let her have this too.*

Tonight, Mrs. Hattingh's reading makes less sense to me than ever—all the words could be one, just a run of sounds stretching and tumbling into one another for all the understanding I have. I'm convinced too that beneath her voice is another sound—of an animal, a cat or snake, hissing, spitting.

I feel woozy from the fire's heat when I see that Rosa is still in here. She's not been taken back upstairs. Mrs. Hattingh has hung her up, and Fatima is here too, standing before Rosa, their eyes locked, their necks seeming to lengthen in unison. Mrs. Hattingh pauses in her reading, follows my stare and smiles: "Eyes, look your last! Mr. Avery is collecting her next week. I thought I'd hang her up in here and enjoy our final days together."

Fatima turns toward us. Rosa's lips part ever so slightly; from across the room and through the paint, I hear her and Fatima say together, *Look, look.*

"Soraya?" Mrs. Hattingh's voice is not unkind. "Are you quite well?"

"I'm just tired, madam."

"Understandable, my dear."

Look. They're both staring at me now.

"Soraya?"

"Madam?"

"We'll stop there, I think." She places a dried flower to mark her page.

"Yes, madam."

"You're distracted. To Bedfordshire as soon as you've raked the coals and set the kitchen straight . . . Poor thing." She reaches out to stroke my hand. "Grief can tire one so."

FOURTEEN

There is one thing that ties me to my right mind: in my room, in secret, late into the dark night or very early in the morning, I've been using my father's qalams, ink and paper. I do not write prayers—I do not have the knowledge. Instead, I take what he taught me to make something else. I draw a letter in the style of our holy script but in the alphabet of theirs, and onto it, around it or next to it, a picture from one of my stories: the seawoman with her eight arms, the woman who made the baby out of soap, the man who bargains with the jinn, the jinn that tumbles down the mountain. Sometimes I write out a sentence from the story and coax the letters into a picture, just as my father used to with a prayer.

It is the only time in all this thick darkness that I feel any relief; my pining for Nour and my kin, my ache for my father, the worry about how to leave the house—all of it recedes. My mind stills from the moment I take up a sheet of paper, feel its weight, stroke its rough surface with my fingertips. I dream too of a moment when, without her seeing, I can slip one of these drawings into the envelope for Nour, along with a note. I could risk that. I could. I must.

In my room, I dream and draw freely, for she has never sought me out here and I know she never will. Not because of her initial promise—I trust her less than ever—but because one night I looked up and saw Fatima standing guard at the door. She turned to nod, then went back to scanning the garden.

She's here right now, Fatima, scattering a line of warning ash at my door, that ember glow pulsing in her stomach. When I finish this drawing, one of a girl standing by a window holding a newspaper in one hand and a match in the other, Fatima says I must rest, save my strength, for we have much work to do soon.

The next morning, I am more alert. I take up Mrs. Hattingh's breakfast tray, and she barely greets me before asking if I've heard about the kerfuffle around next year's election. *She* thinks it's an absolute scandal. The man who is running is "odious, really, Soraya. The worst sort . . . plans to introduce the most draconian measures." She's having a group of like-minded souls around this evening to discuss it, see if they can rally the troops, so to speak. I shouldn't look so uninterested—even if I don't have the vote—because these things affect *everyone*, and this new man is dangerous, very dangerous indeed. She'll speak to me later about supper—nothing too extravagant. There'll be four of them: Mrs. Cunningham and her husband, Mr. Andrew Cunningham ("don't mention the séance in front of him—he's not to know") and a Mr. Cartwright. At the last name, I jolt.

"Mr. Cartwright, madam?"

"Hmm. He's a vegetarian. Rules out meat for four, thank heavens."

"Mr. Cartwright from the Teachers Training College, madam?"

"Top marks! What a memory you have . . . *Oh.* I see just what you're plotting, and the answer is absolutely not. I'm sorry, Soraya, but I won't ask him about Nour's placement over supper. I can't badger my guests about my private charities, not when they're coming to discuss something this grave. My dear, you look as though you're about to cry. Please don't. I couldn't bear it. I tell you what: if the moment presents itself, I'll raise it with him . . . but to be frank, I think you worry about that boy far too much. He didn't even attend your father's funeral. I call that very shabby."

I'm amazed at how late they stay. Mrs. Cunningham keeps saying they should be getting on, but her husband—a portly man with a habit of staring at me when he thinks his wife isn't looking—cuts her off, saying he wants another drink. Mr. Cartwright is a soft-spoken gentleman, and more than once I catch Mrs. Hattingh's eye, silently pleading with her to say something to him about Nour. She returns my look blankly, and I feel my chance slipping away. I'll just have to do it myself—ask how he likes his coffee, then ask about the college. *Find a way. Find a way.* As I refill his cup, I lean down, breath drawn, words ready—

"Goodness, is that the hour? It's nearly eleven o'clock. I should send Soraya to bed. Thank you, Soraya."

I pretend not to have heard her.

"Soraya? Off you go."

If I just turn to him now, say, *Mr. Cartwright, I'm sorry to bother you, but—*

"*Soraya.* You may *go.*"

There's nothing to be done but obey.

She shuts the door behind me, apologizing on my behalf: "Poor thing. Her father passed away a month ago and she's been in such a sad state ever since . . . *So* absent-minded."

The drink, the coffee, both have loosened this gathering, and they're louder than they know.

"I *thought* she looked a trifle wan." That's Mrs. Cunningham.

Think. Think. I'll knock, saying I forgot to clear the coffee cups, offer more pudding, ask about emptying the ashtrays—

"Aha, it's all falling into place now! *That's* the girl whose betrothed you wrote to me about."

It's Mr. Cartwright speaking, and my heart leaps, for I have misjudged Mrs. Hattingh; she's already written to the man, already pleaded on Nour's behalf.

"Yes, *exactly*! I haven't had a chance to thank you in person, Mr. Cartwright."

"Oh, not at all. Easily done."

"Still, you were so discreet about it. The boy will thank us in the long run."

"What's this? What's this now?"

"Andrew, don't be so brusque, dear."

"Not a bit of it, just curious. Sounds as though Mrs. Hattingh's up to one of her good deeds again."

"That's a flattering portrait, Mr. Cunningham. I just asked Mr. Cartwright to look into a little domestic matter for me."

"You're being very mysterious, Alice. Isn't she being very mysterious, Andrew?"

"*Very.*"

"I have it"—Mrs. Cunningham again—"Mr. Cartwright, you're finding Timothy a post here, aren't you?"

"No, but I'd have him like a shot. Fine fellow!"

"Alas. My son is so happy in London. The Cape's not at all his tea."

"But he's still coming to visit, Alice?"
"Oh yes. Yes, indeed, just a few weeks to go."
"Then *what* is it you two have been plotting?"
"Oh, all right. It's this: Soraya—"
"Who is Soraya?"
"Soraya is Alice's *maid*, Andrew. Do keep up."
"I say!"
"*Soraya*—Persian for 'a constellation of stars.'"
"Is it *really*, Mr. Cartwright? I'll ask her about that tomorrow."
"Unlikely she'd know."
"Oh, Andrew, ye of little faith. Anyway, let Alice tell us. Go on, Alice."
"I'm *trying*. Soraya's fiancé, Nour—"
"You know the *name* of your maid's fiancé?"
"I do, Mr. Cunningham. I've always taken a strong interest in those who work in my home. You may want to consider doing the same."
"Perish the thought."
"For God's sake, Andrew. Let her finish."
"Yes. Yes. Do go on, Mrs. Hattingh."
"Thank you, Mr. Cartwright. Soraya's fiancé, *Nour*, is apparently sharp as a tack, working on a farm at the minute, and was all set to go on to Mr. Cartwright's most excellent Teachers Training College next year. Which is just wonderful, but I did wonder about the *timing*. Soraya's just about settling in here, and if he starts up at the college he'd be back in town, and heavens—can you imagine all the to-ing and fro-ing to Heron Place? Lovers' trysts, daydreaming, wedding planning . . . our schedule would fall to pieces, and I've worked *so hard* to get her on track. And it would fall to *me* to police her virtue."
"Very wise. God knows with their appetites."

"*Andrew!* Alice, please forgive him."

"I didn't hear what he said . . . I'll go on, shall I?"

"Yes. *Please.*"

"I thought a small delay of a year, no more, would work wonders for them both; she'll get into the rhythm of being here, and I'm sure he'll gain all sorts of useful experience on the farm. She's assured me that he's very happy there . . . one of the better ones . . . So Mr. Cartwright very kindly agreed to defer Nour's spot for a year or two—though he's not told *him* that, only that there's no space for him at present, that his marks weren't up to scratch; the last thing we need is him badgering Mr. Cartwright here about when a place may open up. *And* it will be a wonderful surprise when he *does* offer him a spot."

"Gosh, you've really thought this through, Alice."

"I have, Helen. And I'm also taking the time to teach her how to read."

"You're so *selfless.*"

"Well, you know my thinking around this—we have a duty of *care.*"

"And in the meantime, if their courtship falls apart, you'll have a maid who won't be running off to get married, leaving you with the bother of finding someone new."

"*Andrew.*"

"What a wicked thing to say, Mr. Cunningham."

"Forgive me. I forget not everyone is as cynically minded as I."

"At any rate, to business," Mrs. Hattingh says to her guests. "How on earth are we going to keep this wretch from getting in? I don't trust him at all."

Mama and I have always disagreed about how quickly I arrive at anger. She says my temper is frightening because it comes unbidden, without warning. But if you were to ask me, I would say that I am slow to it, that things simmer and hum for an age before the boiling point. But once I am in anger's middle, once my voice has taken to new registers and my body feels fit to burst—skin from bone—I know I have moved from one place to the next. When I was little, I would tell her it wasn't me, it was a Gray Woman; that one of them had climbed into my body, raised my temperature, made my mind run in circles, opened my mouth to shout and everything would come out in a crazy whirling jumble.

But my childhood rages are nothing compared with what I feel now.
The water I have been under has drained.
Things are as clear as day.
I am no longer tired.
I can think.
This is why she won't let me leave the house.
Plan.
I must get word to Nour. Tell him what she's done.
Dream.
She will pay for this.
From the far end of the corridor, floating straight toward me, past the walls empty of paintings, is Fatima, mouth set, eyes alight, nodding in agreement.

I get as far as the gate when she sees me.

I'd tried to leave just after taking up her breakfast tray this morning. Tired as I was, I'd not slept a wink last night, and with each passing hour, I'd grown more frightened, more angry. Fatima had lain down next to me, looking sadder than I'd ever seen her. Outside, I was sure the cat's calls were really Mrs. Hattingh's, come to give me more work, read me more books, take more of my life.

I'll slip out, I thought, find any one of the maids or gardeners from the other houses and beg them to send a message home for me, tell Nour Asam that I've found something out, tell him to come see me, for God's sake, come to Heron Place. But before I'd even had a chance to open the gate, she saw me.

What made her go to her window? She never does, but this morning she did. And she did not even need to call out to me, did not need to say a word. All she had to do was look, and I felt her eyes upon me. All she had to do was raise her hand and beckon with her fingers, and I turned, obeyed, walked back into the house. She knew where I was and I knew she was looking.

Once inside, I go back to my daily tasks as though nothing has happened. She waits until we pass each other in the corridor before saying, her voice steady, without a trace of anger, "If you try that again, I'll dock your wage by at least half. Your mother will receive a reduced amount without knowing why. You're welcome to leave the job altogether, of course, but I wonder how you'll find a new place without a reference. You're to stay here, Soraya. I have need of you."

In the days that follow, I make sure that my anger is folded up tightly and comes to life only when I call upon it. I do everything like clockwork, just so, neat, tidy, precise: *good morning*, wake, tea, toast, jam on tray, curtains, wipe, move, cook, *thank you*, sweep, *thank you*, tidy, polish, scrub, *I'm coming*, weed the garden, tea, *good afternoon*, scrub, polish, sweep, wash, dry, fire, fire, fire, *please, I'm sorry, I'm coming*.

Somehow, somehow, I must get a message to Nour about her scheming; he must know what she's done. A single sentence would do it: *Your place at the college was stolen from you.*

How? *How?* Wipe, move, cook, *thank you*, sweep, *thank you*, tidy, wake, *good morning*, tea, *good afternoon*, scrub, polish, *please, I'm sorry, I'm coming.*

The thoughts I used to work so hard to quiet—larks! fancies! bubbling, troubling daydreams!: her head boiling like a crayfish's, watching her slip down the stairs, burning to a crisp in her bed—I let them be as loud as they like while Fatima sighs from a corner of whichever room I am in: *More, more.*

How do I get word to him? A note written on my father's paper, given directly to the postman? To the butcher when next he knocks? But what if either man says something to her?

No. Somehow, I must have a reason to leave the house.

I'm in the kitchen preparing her lunch when it comes to me: if she is hurt or takes ill, I'll have my chance.

Fatima points once again to the rat poison. *Too risky,* I reply. Then, because she keeps pointing, I explain: *A sprinkling would make her ill enough to leave Heron Place, yes, but too much may kill her.*

Fatima just shrugs in response and draws her veil over her face.

"Soraya, will you mend this for me?"

She's holding up one of her nightdresses—pale silk edged with cream lace. The one she wore when I massaged her.

"I tripped getting out of bed this morning. Such clumsiness. I must have dropped some of my face oil on the ground without realizing. Just look at this awful rip. My eyes aren't what they used to be, or I'd do it myself." She waves the spectacles she has taken to wearing on a chain around her neck like the trussed-up limbs of a chicken. "Would you mind terribly?"

"Not at all, madam."

I'd scrubbed her bedroom floors yesterday and poured a little oil by her bed. Not enough, apparently.

"You do such beautiful, fine work."

"I'll take this outside where the light is good."

"I'll come out too. The lavender bushes could do with a prune. Busy hands, Soraya, busy hands."

I am stabbing a needle into the nightdress, weaving a deft line along the rip. When I am done, you will see only the seam on the inside, the scar in the silk.

She is in the garden, just out of sight, behind the bedsheets I hung this morning.

We wrap our dead in white sheets after we have cleaned and prayed over them, wrap them tight so there is nothing between them and the ground but thin cotton. Mrs. Hattingh will be buried in a coffin; it will take longer for the earth to close around her, for her body to rot—longer for her to return, as we each must, to nothing, to everything. Look how she walks, look how she inspects the sheets for stains as though she has done nothing wrong, as though no harm is coming to her. She reaches and touches the back of her neck as though she knows my eyes are upon her; her fingers stray over the pale, freckled skin between the start of her hair and the end of her dress. She turns, sees me and gives a little wave. I wave back.

When I finish the garment, I collect the dried washing and go looking for her. She's in the kitchen, poking around, trying, no doubt, to find fault with something. For a moment I stand in the doorway, the sun on my back, the small linen basket hoisted on my shoulder like a second head.

"Ah, there you are, Soraya. I was just having a little think about lunch."

"I've finished, madam," I say cheerfully, putting the basket down and fishing out her nightdress. She runs a finger back and forth along the new seam.

"Exquisitely done. And nice to see an almost smile from you! I gather you're feeling a little better?"

She holds the nightdress against her person.

"Whatever would I do without you?"

FIFTEEN

She's slipped into one of her solitary states again—fewer guests, less attention to herself, days when she forgets to wear her wedding band and her breath is sour. Puts on no scent. Picks at her food. Stops going to meetings about that man running for election, stops talking about how *terrible* he is, how dangerous. Perhaps, I hope against hope, she'll need me to fetch the doctor. I would have to leave the house, go all the way into town! When I suggest this, she smiles bravely and says no, she'll soldier on, it's just a passing illness.

It's a mercy anyhow: in her quieter moods she asks less of me and I have more time to think. So far, I've been cautious—a little oil placed by her bed, overspiced curry for supper, unboiled milk at teatime—but all that's happened is a torn nightgown and an upset stomach. Angry as I am, I *have* to make it look like an accident. I know their laws and punishments. If I'm caught, if she's truly hurt, it will be the dungeon or the noose for me. Whenever I see her, I smile. I'm cheerful. One face for her.

A few days into her being poorly I find out the reason: Timothy's arrival has been postponed yet again. She shares that he will not be arriving mid-December, two weeks from now; a cough he developed during the war has come back with a vengeance, and since it's wintertime there, he can't risk the journey. She's sad, naturally, but better safe than sorry. She may actually make the trip to *him*; it's something to consider, at any rate.

"I'm sorry to hear he's not well, madam."

"Thank you, Soraya. I'm sure with some rest he'll be on the mend. His lungs were always a little weak—even as a boy. And that stint on the front line made it that much worse." She shuts her eyes and starts to sway a little. "I remember when he wrote to say he was joining the Flying Corps. Anything to get off the ground, he said, anything to get out of the trenches. God, I feel just dizzy thinking about it, even now. It *terrified* me, and I wrote and told him so. He teased that he'd be 'that much closer to God.' Do you believe in God, Soraya?"

"Of course, madam."

"I do admire the simplicity of your people's devotion. But then you're taught not to question, aren't you? *I* always thought the path to God was through inquiry, but in my old age—*now, now*, don't protest, I know I am positively *ancient* in your eyes—I have begun to see God's hand in everything. Daily surprises, small miracles. I had one such miracle today. Can you guess what it was?"

"No."

"Try."

"I couldn't say, madam."

"It will lighten your heart! Is that a good clue?"

"I don't know, madam."

"Oh, you're no fun. I've had a letter from Nour. Your prayers have been answered, even if mine have been deferred."

The rag I'm holding drops to the floor.

"You dropped something."

"Can I have the letter, please, madam?"

"Not this again, Soraya. You know the rules. We'll read it after I've had my supper. Don't purse your lips so. I tell you what: with Timothy's delay, I see no harm in your having a short visit to the Quarter. Our household preparations are nearly complete anyway. Perhaps for an afternoon in the new year. How does that strike you?"

If she's ever eaten more slowly, I'd be hard-pressed to remember it. Each mouthful takes a year; each course, a century. By the time I've cleared the dishes and put out the coffee, we are running an hour later than usual. Fatima has already settled into Timothy's favorite chair, facing Rosa, who looks on, sees all.

From her writing desk, Mrs. Hattingh waves Nour's letter. She's already opened it. "I thought it best I read it first, considering how things stand between you two, and I'm sorry to say that my instincts have been proven correct. My dear, he is not *fit* to be the custodian of your heart or promise. Listen now: 'Dear Soraya, I am sorry I was unable to attend your father's funeral.' Finally! An apology. An admission of wrongdoing! We can be glad of that, I suppose. 'We all, in the Quarter, mourn his passing. We will remember . . .' His handwriting is a little careless here, let me just . . . 'We will remember his goodness and his example . . .' I'd have hoped he'd have something a little more original to offer . . . And now the more difficult bit . . . Goodness, it's hard cheese to be the bearer of bad news. Are you ready?"

"Yes."

"Oh, my poor Soraya. He writes . . . I won't bother to read it off, I'll just sum up: my dear, I'm afraid he is breaking off your engagement . . . He says it's the best thing, that it's not right to make you wait and wait until he earns a place at the college, that he wishes you the best. Really, if you think about it, he's acting quite honorably. Lucky for you that you have a position here . . . I know you'll be heartbroken—'twas ever thus, as they say!—but the days ahead are not without pleasure for either of us. Nour may have abandoned you and my son's visit is a little delayed, but we have the joyful distraction of reading. *Think*. Just us two and the riches of Dickens."

My anger, kept back for so long, floods through me. No more caution, no more care, no more one face for her, another for me. I lunge forward and grab Nour's letter.

"What are you *doing*? Give that back this instant!"

That's it, that's it, chants Rosa, while Fatima glides over to the fireplace, hisses and points to the poker, instructing me to *pick it up* and keep the bitch at bay.

Later, I tell her.

But Mrs. Hattingh is calm, smiling. "Come now. You're not the first girl to be jilted and you won't be the last. Don't be foolish. Give the letter back to me. We won't speak of him again. You can't burn away his words, Soraya."

"I'm not going to burn his letter. I'm going to read it."

She laughs. *Laughs*. "*You're* going to read it?"

"I can read it."

"I don't doubt that by now you can manage a few words. But you won't be able to read it in its entirety. Come now. Hand it over. I'll read it to you."

"*No!*"

"I understand you're upset, but you're behaving abominably. Give it here. *Now.*"

"I know about what you asked Mr. Cartwright to do. I know about you telling him to take Nour's place from him."

"How on *earth*—"

"I *heard* you. I heard you tell your guests about it."

"Listening in at doors? I didn't take you for a sneak. Well, then you should also have gathered that I did it for you. If Nour had any backbone he'd have been spurred on to work that much harder. Instead, he's broken with you."

"Stay where you are."

"How fierce you look. All right. See, I shan't move until you say. I'll sit right here. Go on and read the letter."

"Stop *smiling*!"

I'm amusing her, that's clear. She's not afraid of me. She doesn't believe for a moment I can read the letter or that I'd ever harm her, and I suddenly feel less able to do either. What if I can't make out his handwriting? What if there's something else in it that she's hiding from me, protecting me from? I turn it over, staring at it until she says, "*There.* You can't make hide nor hair of it, can you?"

I read it from start to finish and back again. I'm underwater, blood thumping in my ears, struggling to move, not knowing where to go. A hand pulls me to the surface. It's Fatima. She waits until I've stopped gasping for air and tells me, *Say it.*

I look up from Nour's letter, knowing that the hatred I've felt for Mrs. Hattingh for so long is sane, just. With Fatima beside me and Rosa looking on, I read out loud what he has written.

> Five letters unanswered, Soraya, and not a single message
> sent to me through your family or mine. This is the final

letter I will send. I have asked your forgiveness for not getting
home in time for your father's funeral over and over. I will
not ask it again. I was in the Quarter within the week to do
all your mother needed, all she asked for. Have you even
told her you broke off our engagement before your father's
passing? She has said nothing about it to me. Or about this
man you claim you love. When you first wrote to say we were
finished, I thought it was your shame at my losing my place
at the college and then that it was your grief about losing your
father. I believed you'd come to your senses. This man from
the District—someone none of us know or have even heard
of!—have you made him up just to hurt me? Get rid of me?
Either way, you have been cruel, describing in detail your
love for him. But I am tired of writing, asking, begging you to
reply. Enough. I enclose each one of your lying letters. I do
not want them near me. And know this: I will not return to
the Quarter. When this wretched year is out, I am going to go
north.

Mrs. Hattingh is as white as one of their corpses. "But you cannot. You cannot—"

Say it, spits Fatima.

I pick up the poker, look straight at Mrs. Hattingh and say, "I will kill you."

She's running, running, halfway already to her bedroom while I scream from the bottom of the stairs, "What have you done?! What have you *done*?!"

The edge of her petticoat flashes and skims the landing.

Moments earlier, she'd dashed past me and slammed the door behind her and was halfway upstairs by the time I opened it. Let her trap herself in her bedroom. Let her run circles around it like a headless bird. I'll be slow, say what needs saying, do what needs doing, find what needs finding. I'm still holding the poker in one hand, in the other, Nour's letter, and as I walk, I talk. I'm arranging my mind. I'm working things out. There is no rush. The whole night stretches before us. This night which Fatima, who now walks beside me, so close I can feel her touch for the first time, has long been preparing me for.

In the distance, I hear a key turn and a chair dragged to barricade the door. I can't help but laugh, thinking of all the nights I did the same against Mr. Edenburg's arrival.

That's fine. I can wait her out.

At her desk, I have reason to laugh again, for in her haste to flee upstairs, she's left open the drawer containing Nour's letters: the ones she read to me, the others she hid or he sent back. I drop into her chair.

I must know everything. Everything. I read and read, my skin rising off my bones.

For months, even before my father's death, she had been writing to him in secret. Pretending to be me. Telling him that I had been taught by her to write, to read, that all I said to him was private, between us only. She's lied more boldly than I could have dreamed. Spoken of things that even now make me blush. Letter after letter. And in response his love. Confusion. Worry. Pain. Passion, passion . . . *You write so often and so well about our kisses . . . You say things I would hesitate to . . . the feel of me against you, night dreams of me, your yearning for me asleep and awake . . . That you are able to read and write these days without Mrs. Hattingh's help is an unmatched joy for me. Though I know how difficult that has been, how hard you've worked. But how fine, how very fine, your script has become, my Raya . . . Perhaps one day you will be able to teach others too . . . I am sorry I cannot write several times a week as you have been doing . . . I too crave your company, your being . . . How carefully you recall our life in the Quarter, almost, almost, I feel myself home when I read your descriptions . . . We are unlucky that each time I have a weekend off, you do not . . . Your father, your father, we all loved him so . . . You say that since his passing, you are happier staying at Mrs. Hattingh's than coming home, but I wonder how this can be so . . . My love, grief will not always "hold you by the throat" . . . Come home, come home. Be with your people, share your heartbreak . . . Come home. We will find a way . . . Who is this man you have met? . . . I will not return to the Quarter. When this wretched year is out, I am going to go north.*

I see all the truth of it now. She's made us one and, in doing so, made me nothing. Declaring her love to him as though she were me. Whatever I told her about my home or him, in passing or in earnest—*we pickle loquats, my aunt will make my wedding dress, I have loved him since I was a child*—she has taken to assure him that it is *I* who is writing. It is as though she slipped into my body and under my skin, crawled into my mind and took down my thoughts. Every word is one I would have wanted to write to him but couldn't because she was always standing between us. And she kept me here so that there would be no meeting between me and Nour, no chance of my finding out. Because of *her* I did not know my father lay dying, did not offer him my greetings before death, kiss his hand or his forehead. He left this world without my farewell, without a final blessing for me, so that she could become me, take what was mine for herself, console herself in her loneliness, the hell with my heart, the hell with those I love.

"She has kept me here," I tell Fatima. "Kept me from Nour. Kept me from my kin. Lied to me. Lied to Nour. I may never see him again."

I run toward her bedroom. Grab the doorknob, turning and twisting it, making the door itself tremble, striking it with the poker. "Come out! Come out!" I scream, and when she doesn't obey, when all I hear is a small whimper, I shout some more: "Evil! Evil. I know all! Writing to Nour—pretending to be me. Speaking to him about kisses and longing. *Filthy.* Lying about us. Keeping us from each other, keeping me from my father's bedside. Sending him your son's clothing in secret. When everyone knows that your son cannot stand to look upon you and that's why he never comes back here. What did you do that keeps him so far away? What have you done to make him hate you so? Or does he despise your poverty and your strangeness? Everyone talks about it! All of us. Even the lowest in the city. Come out and *face* me . . . If you don't, you will *see*, I will make you."

I rattle the door again. On the other side, all is quiet, still.

But I know just how to smoke her out.

I go to Timothy's room, and once inside it, I'm awhirl: My hands grab at the bedsheets, seizing, pulling, dumping all on the floor. I tramp my boots over the clean quilt and grab books from the shelf, throwing them all around, with some landing open, pages up, like half accordions. I seize his school uniform and rip off the blazer's badge, topple the miniature soldiers, toss his collection of rocks onto the floor and kick hard at boxes of schoolbooks. I jump on the bed until I'm able to snatch the biplane hanging from the ceiling, breaking its wings before throwing it on the floor. In the room's corner stands Fatima, who looks on, saying nothing, and only once, when I spit on the photograph of Timothy and his friends, does she give a slight shake of her head and turn away.

"Soraya—"

Got her! Mrs. Hattingh is standing not quite in the room, hands covering her mouth, fingers creeping up to her eyes as though she cannot bring herself to see what I have done. I am hot, panting, but I will *make* her see. I take her hands from her face, I peel them from her eyes, and I say, exactly, gloriously, "See what it is like? *See!* To *ruin* what is precious to someone? It was wickedness to pretend to be me! To keep me from my kin. To *use* us so!"

She stands still and mute, as though cast in stone or salt, then her head moves, very slightly, until her eyes lock with mine. It is then that I know I must run. *Run*.

From the bottom of the stairs, I watch as she gets up from where I've pushed her and slips into Timothy's room. I must go home. There is no need to kill her. Instead, I will shame her in front of the city. All of us maids and gardeners, calligraphers, tailors, laborers, teachers-to-be, we will know her lunacy, will laugh and let the story spread like a mountain fire. It will travel from our world into hers, and she will be burned out of existence. The scandal of it! The upstanding Mrs. Hattingh—committeewoman, champion for fallen women, orphans and fishermen, thorn in the side of the governor, tea holder, fundraiser—writing filth in secret to the maid's fiancé. She will never be able to leave the house again. She will die of shame.

"I will tell everyone what you have done!" I scream up before slamming the front door behind me.

Down, down that wide, steep street, the night still and windless.

I stop on the corner, panting, thirsty. My upper lip is damp with perspiration, my blouse uneven. I must look a fright. I hunt through my purse for my handkerchief, and it is then that I realize that I've left all I own behind—clothing, drawings, my father's rakam—and that she's not given me my month's wage, nor has she sent it on to my mother as she promised she would.

The *bitch* hasn't paid me. We may starve because of her.

I will have to go back.

And I am *damned* if she will keep my letters too. I will need them as proof to show Nour. To show the city! In the years ahead people will visit my grave; they will take courage from my life and inspiration from my death, they will plant jasmine at my feet and chant suras near my head. I will snatch back what is mine, and if death comes to either of us this night, I think wildly, so be it. *So be it.* I run through the garden as though the devil is on my heels. In my room I gather my clothing and precious papers.

Back in the house, I make out a faint sound—a low wail, long and guttural. I climb the stairs, legs shaking slightly. The wailing grows stronger, a moan, then a flurry of hard-fought-for breaths. The door to Timothy's room is only slightly ajar. I peek and see first Mrs. Hattingh's stockinged feet, one shoe on the floor, the other on the crumpled bedclothes. I push the door and there she is, her whole body flat on the bed, eyes shut, her hair a crazed halo as though she has been raking her hands through it, on her cheeks two grayish streaks where mascara has mingled with face powder and tears. One hand is placed above her head; the other strikes her chest again and again. Through the rough sobs, she repeats her son's name over and over. All around: books, toppled soldiers, clothes.

"Timothy, Timothy, Timothy."

On the table next to the bed is her little vial of laudanum. If I know her, she has already taken some or is about to. Either way, she will be fast asleep soon enough.

She is in no fit state to speak with me. I will have to get my wages myself.

In the drawing room, I find the small key to her writing desk and tug open the little drawer where she keeps her money. I count out the bills. I will take no more than what I am owed, though how my family will survive without my working for a little while is anyone's guess.

I write a note to her: just one word, *wage*, and the amount I have taken.

A reminder that between the two of us, I am the honest one.

I will date it too.

There. *Lessons learned, madam*.

I pick up my bag. This time, I will leave for good.

Look, someone says softly.

For a moment I worry that it is Mrs. Hattingh come down to fight, her voice hoarse from weeping, but no, it is, I realize as I turn in the direction the voice came from, Rosa, watching, urging.

Look, says Fatima, standing next to Rosa now.

"I have to go," I say. "I'm so sorry to leave you both."

Look.

Look.

"All right." I unlock the remaining desk drawers. There is nothing that interests me, just the old woman's household books.

Look.

Fine. I flip through the account book; something about seeing her bills, what she owes, skimming her balance ledger, witnessing her hardships laid out in pounds and pence, the cobbling and scraping together, the little column titled *Timothy's Monthly Pension*, another for the paltry sum from her late husband's savings, the smallness of each amount, gives me a little shiver of pleasure.

Everything is filed and ordered just as it should be, just as it *would* be with her, *neat, neat, neat*, and I'm about to shut the drawers when I see tucked deep within, right at the back and tied up with a thin navy ribbon, two sets of letters. The first addressed in Mrs. Hattingh's hand to *Lieutenant Timothy Hattingh* in France, the second to her.

Even from here, I can sense Mrs. Hattingh's hunger for me, for Nour, how she snaps at our ankles. I feel her arms reach for us. I must leave and quickly.

Not yet, Rosa and Fatima say, raising their voices to a shout.

"But I've got everything. Money. My letters."

As one, they cast their eyes toward the table.

Fine! I shall read her letters too if that's what they want. Force my way in, unwelcomed, unwanted, just as she has done with me. I walk with my softest tread to the bottom of the stairs and lean to listen: I can no longer hear her weeping. Laudanum or sleep must have taken her. I have some time.

I skim the sentences, hearing, in my mind, Mrs. Hattingh's voice: *Be sure to share your tuck with the men under you. I find that even small gestures of generosity help to build esprit de corps . . . Sometimes I wonder what on earth I'm doing here, in this sun-bright city with its pitchy winds and endless gossiping . . . I worry that I'd be better off at home, closer to you, even if seeing you is an impossibility . . . I will write more after supper . . . When you receive the next letter, it will come with the sum you ask for and more. In the meantime, this one contains newly knitted socks and all my love. Harold Cunningham writes to his mother weekly (clingy) . . . do keep an eye on him and mind yourself.*

One letter is much like another: *Stay Safe. The dahlias have come up beautifully this year. I pray for your return. Whitefish for dinner.*

The second pile is just a sheaf of money orders not from Timothy but from the War Office—I suppose that's his soldier's pension that he sends down to his mother. Beneath that, another letter looks as though she crumpled it in an angry fist and then smoothed it out. The address says it comes from a hospital in England.

That's it, Rosa and Fatima whisper, smiling. *There you go.*

Dear Mrs Hattingh,

Lieutenant Hattingh remains comfortable. I must ask you, once again, to respect our request that you <u>do not</u> attempt to visit your son and to reiterate that if you <u>do</u> arrive at the asylum unannounced and uninvited, you will not be allowed to see him. My staff and I are doing all we can to ensure that he receives the therapies and care—both physical and mental—best suited his injuries. It is regrettable that the methods applied when he first came to us did not take as well as we hoped. While not everyone is able to cope with the rigorous demands of wartime, my colleagues and I have consulted closely, and we agree that Lieutenant Hattingh's silence is elective, indeed, it errs on the side of stubbornness, and that speech will return with the correct pressures and encouragement. I'm afraid I cannot disclose to you what the precise nature of treatment will be (particularly given your continual questioning of our previous decisions), but I can assure you that he is in good hands. I understand—and sympathise!—with your desire to see your boy—my own mother would have felt the same—but I know that if Lieutenant Hattingh were in his right mind, he too would show a soldier's discipline and insist that you stay where you are.

I will write, as ever, with a monthly update on his condition.

Until then, I ask that you slow your correspondence to us.

Sincerely,
Captain Edward James Dalton (M.D.)

PS. Later: I've just returned from my rounds and am pleased to share that physically, Lieutenant Hattingh <u>does</u> show signs of some improvement. As communicated previously, his remaining hand is now able to hold a spoon long enough to bring it to his mouth. In the days before the electric shock therapy, he evinced some enthusiasm when presented with his wheelchair. We hope that when he emerges from this response to the treatment, he'll make further progress. There <u>are</u> some patients who do not take as well to the interventions as we hope, but their minds are a little weaker than most, and by all accounts, Lieutenant Hattingh was a very robust fellow to begin with! In my professional opinion, all he needs is quiet, rest, some firm guidance, a little more <u>will</u> on his part, and he'll vastly improve. Coddling him with visits and an excess of maternal care is ill-advised at this stage.

There are other letters, very short, a few lines at most, written by nurses, telling her how Timothy is: *He had a bite to eat today! . . . Last week we thought he was trying to say something . . . He's been very good. Behaving nicely.*

The most recent one is not a letter but a telegram. This time from the doctor. Sent just a few weeks ago: DEAR MRS HATTINGH

STOP REGRET TO INFORM YOU NO IMPROVEMENT STOP INSTEAD DETERIORATION AND UNWILLINGNESS STOP POOR RESPONSE TO CONTINUED TREATMENT STOP A VISIT FROM YOU BEFORE THE END IS ADVISED STOP NOT LONG NOW STOP A MONTH OR TWO AT MOST STOP APOLOGIES FOR THE BREVITY STOP

My hand has not left my mouth.

My God. My God. Guide me. Guide me.

There is no solicitors' firm. No young lady. No birthday trip to the theater or visit home planned for next month. There is nothing but a boy in a hospital, his body broken, his mind God knows where, his mother spinning stories faster than either of them can speak or dream, his time running out. These letters, *these* are the ones she's been passing off as coming from her son.

Rosa's voice fills the room: *I told you. I told you so.*

I reach for one of Mrs. Hattingh's cigarettes and light it, steadying myself, inhaling the tobacco, feeling its singe to my throat, its bitterness on my tongue. *Easy, easy,* I mutter.

Nour, I think, out on the farm on a cold night, receiving letters from a madwoman, wearing the clothing of a boy hurtling between this world and the next.

That's right, says Fatima.

Fatima shakes out her skirt. The firelight turns the white of her apron the same soft orange as Rosa's scarf. She stands before the painting, her old eyes leaking a little, reaching up to touch Rosa's cheek. I switch back and forth between them: long necks, same skin, old, young, old, young: *Came with the house . . . A gift from the previous owners . . . Worked here since she was a girl . . . Old and gray by the time we bought Heron Place. Came with the house.* I realize for the first time what they have both—ghost and painting, Gray Woman and My Company—tried to tell me again and again: Rosa is Fatima is Fatima is Rosa. That first night that Fatima showed herself to me. That first day I'd wanted to reach up, tear Rosa off the wall and run home with her. One and the same: Trapped here. Trapped here.

"I will take you home," I promise them both.

No need, says Fatima. *But take what is rightful.*

I look down; on my hands, a faint coating of ash as though I have just cleaned out the fireplace or been in a war. When I look up, Fatima is gone and Rosa is no more than a painting.

SIXTEEN

I sink into Timothy's favorite chair, my mind ablaze.

Mrs. Hattingh has been playing with lives, making unholy traffic between the truth and falsehood, taking up my life bit by bit, word by word, and there's been no rest, no rest at all, for the boy who fell from the sky above a faraway desert, who's spent each day of each year since trying to reach home, finding himself barred from entry because she told anyone who would listen, *He is whole, he is fine.*

No rest, Mama, he tried to tell the soothsayer, *no rest for the wicked.*

All this time, I have been cleaning a broken boy's room, laundering his clothing, reading his books. All this time, the monthly sum she claimed was a gift from her boy working so hard in faraway London was, as she wrote truthfully in her ledger, a pension from their government, the smallest sum to a mother in exchange for the body and mind of her son. How she's lied, how carefully she's spun each story—*he will visit soon, he is a solicitor now, there is a young lady*—and how we all believed her, even her friends, too far from the place they all still call home to know any better, too busy tending to their own grief to question her. All this time she's been listening to me, pocketing my stories, imagining herself in my fiancé's bed, shoring up my life against her own. How she's stolen from me, bound me to her, trapped Nour and me. Trapped us.

I need tea, something hot and sweet and steadying to latch me back to this world, and a cup for Mrs. Hattingh too, to return her from where she has traveled, though God only knows where that is and I do not know if it is possible to fetch her whence.

Head full, I walk to the knife-filled kitchen. I wash my hands clean of the ash and reach for the porcelain cups, paying no mind to the mug she set aside for me. I put the kettle on to boil, measure out the leaves, watch them expand, swim, darken the hot water. I must cast salt on the floor, then water over it and sweep; that will drive out some of what clings to this house. I will light the buchu, hold the pulsing orange embers first up to the room's corners, its windows.

I must pray, burn the buchu, cast the salt. The salt dissolves into the hot water and the broom bristles scour the floor, *out, out, out*. I fling open the kitchen door to the night—if only this were daytime, the sun would help to bleach this lying and wrongdoing. But no matter, night or day, I must work to cleanse what I can of this house, I must do what I can to protect myself in my final hours here.

I do not know where this night will take us, only that I cannot leave her or this house just yet. This is not finished between us; there is still work to be done, and an idea, the seed of it, placed by Fatima before she left, is starting to sprout.

I march the tray into the drawing room, and there I take out

Mrs. Hattingh's monogrammed paper and set the rest out: pen, ink, blotter, envelope, knife.

I go to fetch her from his room, recalling the first time I met her, her dress trailing the carpet, hand delicate on the banister, how certain she seemed about the world and her place in it.

She's still on Timothy's bed, wide-eyed, staring at the ceiling, the laudanum untouched.

When she hears me, she bolts up, hands at her sides, eyes swollen, hair in red-gray curls to her shoulders. She lifts her hand to her hair, trying to pin it back, then gives up. "Soraya," she says softly, "Soraya." She looks about her, at the mess, at the toy soldiers on the floor, and weeps afresh. "Soraya . . . his room. His *room*. Timothy, my boy, Master Timothy . . ."

I turn to say plain and clear, "I know all. I know about Nour. I know about Timothy. He's been only half alive all this time. And he may be *dead* soon."

I pronounce both *d*'s as though they were the ends of his coffin and the letters between were his body, laid out, covered up. At this word she springs toward me and puts a hand over my mouth. "Hush. Hush . . . no more of that. We must clean up his room. Pick up the books. Fold his clothes. Quickly now." She reaches for Timothy's garments herself, makes a pile of them on the bed. She picks up a jumper, smooths it out, folds the arms back. "Look," she says as she hangs the final shirt. "This shirt has lost a button."

Though my tongue is thick and dry, I say, "He's in a hospital. Can't even feed himself. Or talk."

On her knees, she crawls on the carpet until she finds the button. "Where's the needle? The thread? Where have you put it? We must sew this back this instant." She opens drawers, scratching through them, turns over scattered books and bedclothes. "Not here."

"They're doing all manner of things to him in that place. And you are here."

She sees his school blazer at her feet, bends to pick it up, dusts it off, holds it to herself. "Did you see the boys, Soraya, when they came back? Half a leg, eyes gone, shaking at the slightest sound?"

I'd seen them. We all had. There were boys from the Quarter who'd fought their war too, given no weapons, undefended, who'd come home maimed, lost their minds and limbs on burned-out fields green with gas. Some left their souls there too, tangled up in barbed wire, dying on their battlefields.

"I knew if I shared that he was injured with anyone, they'd assume the worst, just as you have."

"What?"

"Everyone buried the boys alive, carved their names on plaques, gave them no chance to come back." She stares at me. "And I was *right*. I was *right* to do what I did. He'll get better. See again. Speak again—"

"But you lied. There was no job in London."

"I said he was at Langridge's, the same place offered by his commanding officer. Just as we planned. He'll be there soon enough. Not a matter of if but when." She leans into the wardrobe, inhaling whatever smell is left of her boy, voice stripped and soft. "And in the meantime, you've been here. My company and my comfort."

An image of my mother comes to me, of her holding tight to my sister, Mama's face wet on her child's shroud even as the women of the Quarter prized Baby gently, gently away. Another, of my father, his breath rasping as he lay in his bed, waiting for me, waiting for Kashif, begging Death for a few moments more, bargaining, *My children are just a few streets from here. I know it.* He reminds Death that we need to kiss his forehead and he our hands, that he must give us a final blessing before he travels from this world to the next. My father, deprived of his farewell, his children deprived of theirs. My mother today, sitting in the kitchen, kept apart from her eldest child, the one who should be returning home weekly to run the house, feed the children, see off the neighbors if it all became too much. Instead, I am *here*, with the person who had my brother sprinting across town while our father lay dying, held captive by her sorrow, being asked to listen to her stories, forgive her sins, offer her comfort, spend all the hours of my days, my life, with her.

"As for writing to Nour, well, I did that as a kindness to you . . . Slowly at first. Just a few sentences, poorly conceived with even worse penmanship, full of errors, just as you would have done. And then, in increments, so subtle he'd barely notice, I improved. For a while he received the most beautiful love letters from you. Declarations of fidelity. Dreams for your future. I did what I could to strengthen your courtship. Built an oasis in a desert. You should be grateful, not brimming with outrage. I even sent him my son's jumper because he mentioned once that the nights were growing colder. A kindness you now wield against me. Don't blame me for how weak and feckless he is, running at the slightest hint of difficulty. Don't you see, Soraya"—she grabs my hand and hangs on to it—"I've exposed how little he really cares for you. How un*willing* he is to fight for you. You must stay with me, my dear. It's better here. Better here."

I wrest my hand from hers. "You will not speak of Nour again. And you must listen to me. I have a task for you."

"*You* have a task for me?"

"Yes. We have work to do."

"Have you gone mad?"

"Maybe. But you must come with me now."

"And if I refuse?"

I do now what she has so often done with me: I make my voice soft-soft, and I stare out past her as though I am somewhere else, saying things as though they are not threats but musings.

"To me," I say, as though making conversation, "gossip and fire are the same. A pair. Because they get faster and stronger as they go. And they can make a person's whole life go up in smoke. Do you ever worry, madam, about Heron Place catching alight? I do. All the time. There is paper stuffed in every window. The wood is so stripped and dry. And the mountain with its mad winds just behind us . . . It would take so little for the house to be gone. Just one match and a few breaths . . . Gossip too is wild and fast. Imagine if everyone in the city knew about how you've schemed, writing love letters to Nour, lying about your son . . . Your face would burn hotter than your house.

"And where would you hide," I continue wonderingly, "with your house burned down?"

She leans back, her eyes two slits; she's always been a canny one. "What is it you want?"

At last, I think, we understand each other.

"The week's writing hour, madam. It must be met. Come."

I lead the way out the room, glancing back over my shoulder, making sure she is following.

The night circles close. I light each of the drawing room's candles. Then I point to the desk, saying, "Sit."

She is stooped, smaller; her eyes are aglitter. I watch, without aiding her, as she grabs on to the chair's back and almost falls into the seat. I stand myself behind her. She turns around, still wanting to tell me what to do, but I speak over her, instruct her to drink the tea I have prepared. She shakes her head no; the cup and its contents frighten her, I can see that, but I insist, firmly, that she must have it, that she needs her strength, for there is an important task at hand, and as an act of good faith, I take a sip first. There, I think, we have shared a cup.

She stares hard at me and takes a drink of tea. I say that I have always admired her penmanship, that the beauty of her cursive rivals my father's calligraphy. "Oh yes," I say, when she looks puzzled. "My father was a calligrapher. But he wrote only for his Maker. You will write for me, and this time you will write only what I say. I will be watching, so you must obey."

She nods and, with a shaking hand, takes a single sheet of paper, writing as I command.

Dear Mr Cartwright,

I made a grave error in asking you to defer Mr Nour Asam's place at the college. I pray that it is not too late to rescind this decision for the coming academic year. I would consider it a personal favour if you did this.

Yours faithfully,
Mrs Arthur Wilmont Hattingh
(Alice)

She finishes and looks at me expectantly. I lean over her, my breath hot and close to her neck, and read it through.

"Good," I say, and when she tries to get up, I put my hands on her shoulders, pressing just a little. "Date it. Now place it in an envelope. Address it."

If I narrow my eyes a little, I can see Mama, Lia, Alma, Kashif, all gathered around a table, candles lit, our plates piled high. Nour greets us from the front door, the day's teaching behind him.

She asks if there is anything else, if she can go.

"Not yet. Rosa will leave Heron Place soon, yes?"

"Mr. Avery fetches her in a few days."

"Your company will be gone."

"Yes."

"Tell me again how much she will sell for."

She names the sum.

"And you still don't know who she was." I say this as fact, not question.

"What?"

"Nothing. There is one more letter to write, and then we'll be done. Listen now: 'I, Alice Hyacinth Hattingh, will give the proceeds from the sale of my painting named *Rosa*, overseen by Mr. Samuel Avery in London, to my faithful maid, Soraya Matas—'"

"No! *No*. I have need of that money."

"'This is my wish and a mark of my gratitude for all she has done for me.'"

"But I will have *nothing*!"

"You will have your house. You will have your face."

She understands the threat, that is certain. She puts her pen down and stares at her hands before saying, "All right. I will do as you ask. Not for myself, but for my son. He will need both the house and my intact reputation to return to." She folds her arms across her chest. "But I have something to ask of you in return."

"Go on."

"You must promise not to tell Nour about the letters either—"

"I can't do that!"

"Tell him it was grief that drove you from him. It would not be a lie. Please. I *beg* you. I cannot bear the humiliation. You will have all you need. All you could ask for. You could leave tomorrow, and as soon as I have the money from Mr. Avery, I will send it to you in the Quarter."

I have seen her in all her moods and tempers, but never this, never small. I do not answer directly; instead, I smile a little and incline my head without promising her anything, and just as I suspected she would, she takes from it what she wants.

"*Thank* you, Soraya. I am indebted to you."

I move in close, stand right behind her, repeating the letter to Mr. Avery, watching to make sure she does just as she is told.

"It is a new beginning," I tell her, and place one hand on her shoulder, close to her neck. She reaches up to lace her fingers tightly through mine. There we stay, looking at the sealed letters, and I tell her what my father would always tell me before he wrote his prayers: that beginnings are sacred, a small glow in a dark room, the breath before the verse. The breath before the verse.

The breath, I say to her now.

The breath.

The breath before the verse.

PART III

SEVENTEEN

My dear Soraya,

It is likely that by the time this letter reaches you, my son will have passed on. For several days now, he's been drifting between this world and the next, still without speech but not—and I am adamant about this—without feeling. There are hours when I look upon his face—and I look at all of it, the intact eye, the empty socket, the still-hearing ear, one cheek smooth, the other shriveled—and I can sense all he wants to tell me. It became evident last week that he would not last out the month, and since then, the doctors have allowed me to see him every day. (Or perhaps they realised that come rain, sun, wind or hail, I'd continue to stand each morning at the asylum gate and ring and ring and ring the bell, and if no one came to open it, I'd drag a stick back and forth across the rail, making a racket until someone, anyone, did.)

That first visit . . . where do I begin? The nurse led me to where all the chairbound boys had been wheeled, turned to face the sun and a rose garden in half bloom. She cautioned me that I may not recognise my boy, and it took all my self-will not to slam my umbrella into the back of her head. Not recognise my boy? I, not recognise my boy? Then she said I should also not assume that my son would recognise me.

That first hour with Timothy I said very little, just stroked his broken face, breathed in the smell of his hair, held his remaining hand. I could not bring myself to look at his legs, still and useless (the doctors told me that his not walking is 'simply in his head'). No tears, I told myself, not in front of him, and since then, I've watched other women—mothers, sisters, wives, a few stubbornly faithful girls—do the same. We none of us can understand quite what happens here and why the boys come in still speaking, moving, and then either leave very obedient or remain here without speech or mobility. But we've become our own little band, we women, and we do for one another what we can: some of them live far away and can't always get down, and on those days, I'll sit a little while with each of their men.

I'm close by, you see—I've taken a room in a bedsit just a few streets from the asylum. It is small—smaller even than your room at Heron Place—the gas meter gobbles up coins and the downstairs tenants are a loud, belligerent lot, but the woman who runs it is kind, if a little careworn. We have struck up a friendship of sorts, and she has agreed that if I do the downstairs dusting and help prepare the other tenants' tea, I can pay a reduced rent. I will need the adjustment, for I have decided to live out my remaining days here. I will not return to the Cape, even after Timothy is no longer with us. I understand now that it is this place, not the colony, but this place, with its grey seasons and narrow streets that lead me daily back and forth, back and forth, between Timothy and a little room, that is my home. More, I cannot leave the place my child will one day be buried . . . Grand old Heron Place . . . the sale will finalise soon, for less than I'd hoped—its structural decay was deeper, apparently, than I understood, and the new owners have declared the remaining furniture 'old and worthless'. So it's not the sum I'd imagined, but it is enough to pay the debt of traveling here and of staying on. They have plans, I'm told, to gut the house, tear up the trees and build a swimming pool . . .

Soon, Soraya, there will be no trace left of me in the Cape.

And so I have a final request to make of you: go to Heron Place soon, please—before it's too late!—ask the new people for a cutting of Timothy's lemon tree before they uproot it and plant it in your yard. It may whither in a few weeks, or it may grow sturdy and fruitful. We cannot know. I ask only that you try.

It is one thing, you see, to remove all trace of oneself from a place, another to do the same for one's children. I don't ask this for the sake of 'memory'. (Now that I am here, I am wholly unconvinced by this frenzy of remembering the 'glorious dead'. Everywhere I look, a plaque, a statue, a bride's bouquet, a sputtering candle, an homage of some sort that has nothing at all to do with the broken boys in the rose garden.) I ask because I believe he must have some tie to the place in which he was born. Perhaps years from now you will pickle the fruit, or one of your children will find its yellow sourness refreshing on a hot day.

I do not know if I am asking too much of you.

Do not tell me if you do or don't do it. At any rate, I know not to expect a reply.

I will not write to you again.

Sincerely yours,
Alice Hyacinth Hattingh

The letter is dated two months ago. I place it in my lap and shut my eyes against the sun. See now a door closing, a handful of soil flung on the grave, a vase of flowers placed next to a photograph, a prayer offered up for that boy who'd been frozen in the night sky for so long. Above him, the fire of an exploding plane; beyond that, a dome of stars; beneath, the desert; and ahead, if he's allowed, the long, slow walk to the end, to the beginning.

Alice Hattingh's request swirls all around me: a tree for her son, planted in my yard, its fruit one day to be eaten by my children, to flavor my food. She's never understood the scale of what she wants and asks for. Enough.

I will think on the favor later. For now it is enough to know she will stay there, in that small room, far from the fever dream of the Cape, far from the lives she and hers have spun here out of gold dust and spite.

And I will remain here, in my parents' house, where Rosa's money continues to ease our path and will do so for many years to come. My days are spent mostly in my father's room, my hours a near copy of his: I sit at his desk where the sun angles just so, heating my face in the morning, warming my toes in the afternoon, my head bent, fingertips dyed blue and black with ink. There is not a day when I do not feel Papa's presence, when he does not announce himself through the smell of jasmine or the guidance of my hand on a difficult letter. It is not prayers I write, though I pray constantly while I work. Instead, just as in those first secret hours at Heron Place, I draw the images of my childhood stories and the ones that come to me now. But more, I make an image out of the very words of the stories themselves: if I draw a flower, a man seated by a cool stream, the outline of our mountain ablaze with flowers or fire, the cut of the ocean or a woman dancing on a knife's edge, I do so by bending the words of the story, making all the sentences into a single image. From a distance you cannot tell they are words, but up close, you can follow the story as it moves and curls against the page. Even if you cannot read, I reason, you will still know what it is about.

People come from across the city and beyond to see my drawings, for news travels thick and fast about them. It is not the work of my father (I am not given to that kind of devotion), but it is the work of my life: the Lodge, the Women—Sea, Soap and Gray—all and more are present. There are other stories too, new to me, known to others: of women at wells and men picking fruit, of set-to-work children and long-ago arrivals. Sometimes elders from the Quarter and the District look at these and say, *That is my mother's, my father's, my grandmother's story*. One day I drew a small servant girl reaching for a grape from a glistening silver bowl, her hand trembling, the desire for the sweet fruit stronger than the fear of the beating she and I knew would follow. My mother saw that image and froze, her own hand shaking as she held the page, asking me how I came to this memory of hers from so long ago.

And I am amazed too by this: when my mother brings me my meals, as she did my father, she stays for a few minutes as she used to with him. We none of us ever knew what was said during those moments together, but I know now: she would tell him, as she tells me now, what she thought of the work he was doing. She places her hands on my shoulders and massages them, giving me release and comfort and the gift of more time, the will to work. She draws a line between the work before me and the work already done: *this flower here is too much like that one*; *In this image, the balance is not good*. She speaks simply, but her eye is clear, and I see now her hand in all his prayers. One day I say this to her, and she waves it away, says I am talking such foolishness, but there is a dip to her head, shy as a girl in a schoolroom, that I have never seen before. In the weeks ahead she will pull out the work my father never sold, and she will say, hesitatingly, *In this one, I suggested he write our most holy prayer in the shape of our most sacred building, and here, this one is the first time he wrote in miniature so that the prayers could fold up in a talisman.* When she shows me these things, it is as though I am alive twice: there is the life I have lived, unaware, unseeing, and then there is this one, where I must travel back, pick apart my memories, recast the fullness of my father's gifts, discover my mother's hand in all that he did. I no longer ask which pieces she helped him with; I ask now which she didn't. It is new, this knowledge, that my mother was not just the woman who washed our floors and cooked our meals, but also a person who created alongside my father and then hung back to spin a mist of silence around it all.

I try to make up for this by telling everyone how much my mother helps me: I can see that many do not believe me; they think it is a kind of petting indulgence, that I am being kind to a widow, trying to give her a new life's purpose, and my mother is partly to blame because she adopts an expression of dull bewilderment as if I am making up stories just as I did in my childhood. It is only when the visitors leave that she tells me not to say anything, that no good can come from sharing everything, that half the mystery of life is not understanding how things come into being. Perhaps she is right.

I achieve a kind of fame, I suppose, in this city, for it is not only my own people who come to see the work, to buy it; the settlers come too. They make their way to our neighborhood from their own. Sometimes they live just a street away but act as though they have entered another world and must be applauded for it. It is mainly those who care for artists (or those who like to think of themselves as such); the women arrive in cloches and capes, the men have short, pointy beards and suck on pipes of tobacco while they look over my work. They turn to one another and say, as though I am not in the room, *Fascinating. See how she has integrated the traditions of the Mohammedan but broken the rules of nonfigurative representation . . . And how she has unwittingly taken the form of the East and been inspired by the beauty of the Cape's surrounds?*

By which I suppose they mean I have taken my father's father's father's way and made things about my home. These people, I tell Nour, ever want praise for stating the obvious. I cannot always bring myself to sell the drawings: I wait and watch to see how much they say about them. If they talk too stupidly, I tell them that the work in fact is not for sale. I pretend a superstition I don't hold and say that this painting or that drawing holds special meaning and cannot be moved from the Quarter or *else* . . . I finish with a face that hints that all would be beyond my control if it was. In response, they exchange those wise, amused looks their people are so good at. I can see it already—the tale being turned over, polished, made into something more than it was for a supper party or a letter home.

I thought the house would be quiet in these months after my father's passing, that once the rush of visitors offering condolences and care was done, we would settle into loneliness, that my mother would be left to her grief, but it has not been so at all. Visitors come by every day, and my mother always greets them loudly enough so that I know who is here and I have the choice to come out or hide in my work. And I have found that something wondrous has happened: the anguish of those early days has lessened; I find that I do not need to cower in this room. Ever since I began this work, I am quick to laugh, eager to be with others. I look at my neighbors and I see them as I did when I was a child, see the kindness in the plates of food they bring to us, the sincerity of their greetings. I see the marvel now, that we, who have been ripped to pieces so many times over, who have known such darkness, can still spin and sew lives of such brightness, make music that fills the streets, sing prayers that ring out over the entire city; that we find ways to say over and over, *We are here! We are here!*

When the day's work is done, I make my way to the stoep as I'm doing now. I sit here in the early dusk with Nour, and we speak of the day just passed and the ones to come. If we reach deeper into the past, we dwell mostly on the wild, free days of our childhood. Alice Hattingh we mention only briefly, if at all, for we both know the summoning power of talk. We are concerned with our own lives, our own people. When I ask Nour about school, his face will pull tight and wary, and he'll talk about how he and the other teachers are busy-busy, organizing into groups to get strong for the long fight that lies ahead. For that man Mrs. Hattingh and her friends worried over has been elected by the settlers, and I trust him less than the others—and I trusted the others not at all. He has the look, I tell Nour, with his small spectacles and clean-shaven chin, of a doctor who wants only to cut and hurt. His picture is in all the newspapers and in the advertisements handed out on the street, and whenever I'm given one, I study his face as though it is something I may draw before I throw it in the nearest dustbin. I have found over the years that I can gauge at a glance what someone is plotting, what that person is capable of. And I know, as the talk turns more wicked than ever, to fear this man.

So I do not take these days of drawing and food for granted, these days when I can sit at a table with Mama, Nour, Lia, Alma, Kashif, our plates full, our door open to those in need, these days where what has sat in my chest for all my life has been stilled, soothed. In the dusk on the stoep, before the descent into the dark, I am alive, I am grateful.

But as the athaan sounds out from the mosque, as the street empties out, I too take my leave of the day.

Inside, my family and I prepare for sunset prayers: we pour fresh water into basins, wash our hands up to our wrists, thrice rinse our mouths, our nostrils, our faces, forearms, run wet hands through our hair, behind our ears, wash feet to ankles, declaring together our faith, our witnessing. Soon, we will fall to our knees, touch our heads to the floor, greet our God and our angels. Later, we will sit in the gathering twilight, one eye fixed on the past, the other turned toward the future, and we will pray and plan again and again, for our safety, for our freedom, for the fever here to break, for the fever here to break.

Let it break, I will beg, *Ya Rab!* let it break.

ACKNOWLEDGMENTS

I am so very grateful to Leila Davids, Rachel Holmes, Yewande Omotoso, Barbara Boswell, Carole DeSanti, Dorothy Driver, Lucy Caldwell, and Jill Crawford for reading early versions of what would become *Cape Fever*—every bit of feedback and encouragement seemed to come at exactly the right moment. Thank you to the beautiful Backburners and Hibiscus Salon for writing community and joyful gathering. Cape Town teems with extraordinary artists and thinkers who dream constantly about how to construct the city's past and imagine its future, and I want to acknowledge especially the brilliant, expansive work of Jay Pather, Ilze Wolff, Gabeba Baderoon, and Thania Petersen in this regard. Thank you to David Ricketts for bringing the personality, and to Yusuf and Shereen Davids, whose love creates home.

    I would not have started (or finished) this book without residencies at Hedgebrook, where radical hospitality and magic converge; and at Aspen Words, where I experienced the warm welcome of Adrienne Brodeur and her team and the wondrous generosity of Isa Catto and Daniel Shaw.

I'm so grateful to Olivia Taylor Smith at Simon & Schuster for asking the deepest questions with the lightest touch, for brilliant editorial insight, publishing nous and personal generosity. My special thanks also to Brittany Adames and Sophie Missing for their welcome and enthusiasm. Thank you to the exceptional, eagle-eyed production team: Douglas Johnson, Nancy Tan, Jayne Yaffe Kemp, Valerie Pulver, Beth Maglione, Amanda Mulholland, Lauren Gomez and Olivia Perrault, and to Martha Lanford and Emily Farebrother for planning the voyage out.

My warm thanks to Charles Buchan, Bonnie McKiernan, Sarah Watling and Rebecca Nagel at the Wylie Agency—each has been unwaveringly supportive over the years, treating my work with protective care and dignity.

I'm grateful beyond measure to my husband, John Gutierrez, whose support, love and stubborn faith (even now) make so much possible, and to our children, Ilyas and Sasha, who fill my world.

This book is dedicated to my grandmothers, Amina and Mary: with my love and with my thanks.

ABOUT THE AUTHOR

NADIA DAVIDS is a South African playwright and novelist and a winner of the Caine Prize for African Writing. *Cape Fever* is her debut novel in the United States. She lives in California.